FIRE IN FROST

ALICIA RADES

Published by Crystallite Publishing.
Produced in the United States of America.
Edited by Emerald Barnes.
Cover design by Clarissa Yeo of Yocla Designs.

To Linda Joy Singleton, whose writing I have looked up to for years.

CHAPTER 1

My knees buckled and my hands trembled as I reached for the door to the school. An invisible weight came crushing down on my lungs as I gasped for air.

"What's wrong?" Emma asked with urgency. "Crystal, you look sick. Are you okay?"

I paused, unable to move or speak because I was afraid I would collapse if I did. The truth was, I didn't know *what* was wrong with me.

"Crystal," Emma prodded, resting a hand on my shoulder.

I blinked a few times and finally caught my breath. My voice was hoarse and barely there. "Yeah, I think I'll be alright. I just have a weird feeling."

Once I found my legs, we entered the building. The commons took on a different role today. Instead of everyone seated at tables waiting for the bell to ring, most were crowded toward the far end of the room. It was quieter than normal, too, as if a tragedy had just taken place.

"What's everyone doing?" I asked in a near whisper as I stood on my toes to get a better look.

"I don't know," Emma started, but she cut off. "Oh, yeah. Remember the fundraiser they're doing today for Olivia Owen? They must have started already."

Now that Emma pointed it out, I remembered yesterday's announcements reminding students about a fundraiser in memory of Olivia. I knew Olivia's story. In a small town of 3,500, *everyone* knew about Olivia's tragic death that happened last year.

I approached the table where the crowd stood and moved to the side so I could see. When I got a clear view, I saw two girls sitting behind the table, Kelli Taylor and Justine Hanson, the co-queen bees of the school. Athletic, beautiful, straight A students, these girls were pretty much the poster children for perfection. In front of them sat boxes of candy bars they were selling for the fundraiser.

Informational flyers and pictures of Olivia scattered the table. There was even a large framed photo of her junior volleyball picture taken just weeks before her death. She stood with a confident stance in her number 17 volleyball jersey with the ball resting on her hip. Her blonde hair was straightened, and her dark brown irises made her eyes appear larger than they should. She looked more like an angel than a student. *It's sad*, I thought, *that she didn't live long enough to finish the season—or even to graduate for that matter.*

I grabbed one of the flyers from the stack and began reading.

Fundraising for Burn Victims: In Memory of Olivia Owen

By Justine Hanson

Olivia Owen was once a loving daughter, student, and athlete. She was a straight-A student who set an example for her fellow classmates by becoming an active member of the student council and the community service club. Her athletic abilities surpassed those of her fellow junior-year volleyball players despite her asthma, and if she would have made it to the end of the season, she would have undoubtedly claimed the title of MVP. Olivia was a spectacular human being, volunteering when she could, helping the community with things like the Peyton Springs Halloween Festival and the Fourth of July Parade.

But more than anything, Olivia was my best friend. I knew her and loved her like a sister, and it pains my heart each day to know that her life was cut short at only age 17. When Olivia forgot to blow out a candle before she fell asleep, her curtains caught fire, and she suffered an asthma attack before she could escape the smoke or find her inhaler. I can't imagine the physical pain she must have endured that night.

Because of this tragic tale, Olivia's family and friends decided to honor her life by helping raise money for other burn victims and their families who have survived house fires. Today, on the anniversary of Olivia's death, we ask you to contribute by purchasing one of our fundraising products (candy bars, baked goods, and other donated items) or by simply dropping $1 into one of our donation jars located throughout the school.

Olivia's mother and her friends thank you for any and all contributions, and we hope to continue raising money for families like Olivia's. Thank you, and God bless!

"What's it say?"

I jumped. I didn't realize Emma had followed me to the table.

"It's just a flyer explaining the fundraiser," I told her.

Olivia's story was sad. I felt like I couldn't just leave the

3

flyer there, one that told her story to the world. I wanted to contribute in some way, but I didn't have any money on me, so I simply folded the paper up and slid it in my pocket, hoping that would show I cared.

The thought of death crushed my heart, so I kept my eyes down, avoiding gazes so I wouldn't tear up. I didn't know Olivia that well, but since we were both on the volleyball team—although she was Varsity when I was on the freshman team—I'd spoken to her a few times.

I blinked back tears as I thought of Olivia's tragedy. The whole idea of death brought a lump to my throat and resurfaced memories that I thought I'd gotten over. Emma rubbed my back to comfort me because she knew the subject of death was a touchy one.

As I stared at the floor, afraid to look up for fear that tears might start falling, an invisible force—something unknown willing me to look—pulled my chin up. My gaze fell upon the empty hallway to the right of the commons area where students hadn't yet been released to roam for the day.

In the middle of the hallway stood a tall, beautiful girl with blonde hair and dark brown eyes. She looked at me across the distance, her eyes full of emotion. I couldn't pinpoint exactly what she was trying to say with her expression, except that I knew it was urgent.

As soon as I spotted her, the bell rang, announcing that students could now go to their lockers and prepare for class. The crowd dispersed from the commons into the hallway and blocked my view of the girl. The students hurried down the hall as if they didn't see her. I kept my eye on where she was standing, but I didn't see her again.

"Crystal." Emma's voice seemed far off, a distant hum in my confusion.

The faintness I felt just moments ago returned. My heart

pounded in my ears, and for a second, my knees felt unstable. I gripped the edge of the fundraising table for support.

Emma snapped her fingers in front of my face. "Crystal," she said again as her voice came back into focus.

I was suddenly whipped back into reality, dazed. "Wh —what?"

"Are you okay?" Emma asked with a tone of serious concern. "You look like you've seen a ghost."

I let the statement sink in for a moment. "Yeah," I said. But I wasn't answering her initial question. I was agreeing with her latter statement.

But I didn't see a ghost. I couldn't have. An odd sensation stirred as a chill spread from my spine to the end of my fingertips. This was the same type of chill I used to get when I had my imaginary friend Eva over for tea before I started kindergarten. *I'm imagining things*, I told myself, mostly as reassurance.

But I had seen her clear as day. Olivia Owen had stood in the hallway and begged for my help with nothing but an expression. Yet how could that be when she died a year ago?

Emma took my arm and led me to our lockers as I silently assured myself I wasn't crazy.

CHAPTER 2

*A*s we neared our lockers, I rationalized what I had seen.

Whatever bug I'm catching sure is making my imagination run wild.

I took a deep breath, willing my bad mood to go away, but a tension headache was already forming. I tried putting Olivia out of my head. Easier said than done.

We arrived at our first class, which was my favorite class of the day because it was the only one where Emma, Derek, and I had class together. Plus, Mr. Bailey always left us to our textbooks and let us talk with our group. Needless to say, there was more goofing around than working on geometry homework.

I walked in with a frown on my face. Derek noticed immediately. I moved my desk so it was facing my two best friends, forming a triangle so that we could get to work.

Derek shifted in his chair and looked up at me. "What's wrong?" he asked gently, obviously concerned.

"It's just not a good day," I murmured. With that, I actually opened up my textbook and began reading.

I could see Derek's expression out of the corner of my eye as he looked to Emma for an explanation. She simply lifted her shoulders and opened her own textbook, but I could still see her stealing glances at him.

I apologized for my behavior when the bell rang, but I still couldn't shake off my mood. I seemed to walk through the hall in a daze, blinking back tears and cursing the knot that was forming in my chest. Was I getting sick, or was it something else altogether?

When lunch rolled around, I quietly found my spot next to Derek and Emma at our usual table. We normally sat with the other JV volleyball players but mostly kept our conversations to ourselves. Derek was freely welcome at our table. Last year when he tore his ACL in basketball, Emma and I begged him to join the team as our manager.

Besides, he didn't really have the typical basketball player physique. He was shorter than most of the other players, although his attractive bright blue eyes and curly brown hair made him blend in with the other good-looking guys at school. He hung out with Emma and me more than any other guy, though.

Emma and Derek were arguing next to me about some issue I didn't care to weigh in on, so I blocked them out as I picked through my food. When I lost interest in it and glanced up, I noticed the long table set up against the far wall of the commons.

Kelli and Justine sat behind it, still selling candy bars and taking donations. I watched in awe as they ran their campaign and encouraged passing students to purchase a candy bar or to spare a few pennies. The way they held themselves bit at my own self-esteem.

Our school wasn't very big. In a small town like Peyton Springs, you couldn't expect a large high school. Everyone knew everyone else here. It was so small that some of our team members—like Emma—had to double up on JV and Varsity.

I had talked to Justine and Kelli in volleyball once or twice, but they still intimidated me. Not only were they seniors and at the top of the social hierarchy, but they were gorgeous. Kelli was petite like me, but she'd had more time to fill out, and her gorgeous smile reflected her confidence in her beauty. Justine had a similar smile painted on her face, but her body was one to *really* be jealous of. She had long, slim model legs that she kept in shape with volleyball and weight training, and her tan skin and shiny dark hair had me cursing my pale skin and plain dirty blonde locks.

I had zero curves to speak of and a pencil-shaped body that puberty had not yet had a chance to fill out. I was willing to bet I was the only girl in my grade who hadn't started her period yet. Granted, I was one of the younger students in the sophomore class with a summer birthday. I was nearly a year younger than Emma, who already had her driver's license, but that wasn't any excuse for the universe to slow down the onset of my menstrual cycle.

I wanted to hate these girls. I really did. As much as their mature bodies and full confidence bit at my self-esteem, I couldn't hate them. They'd always been friendly to me. I didn't have any legitimate reason *to* hate them.

I was still watching them when Kelli's boyfriend, Nate, came up to her from behind and embraced her. She flinched at first in surprise. Then she tilted her head back to nuzzle against his shoulder. From this distance, they seemed to make a great pair. They were the designated "It" couple of the school, the two everyone thought would last long after high school. They looked good together, too, with her small but athletic frame and his tall, muscular body. Their blonde hair and blue eyes complemented each other. I couldn't help but take note of how I'd like a boyfriend like that.

While admiring the girls, my mind thought back to Olivia. What would it be like if she were still here? Would she be sitting at that table with them fundraising for some other good cause?

My thoughts drifted back to those I was trying desperately to suppress. *Did I really see Olivia this morning?*

No, I thought, poking at my spaghetti. *I was just stressed and had an image of her face fresh in my mind. I have a wild imagination,* I rationalized. *I don't really know what happened this morning. I'm just remembering it wrong,* I told myself.

With all these thoughts racing around in my head, I hadn't noticed how much time had passed. The buzz of the bell pulled me from my reverie, and I sprang up in surprise. I pushed through the crowd and dumped my tray of uneaten food. Before I let it all fall into the garbage, I grabbed the piece of garlic bread and shoved it in my mouth. I knew if I didn't eat something, I'd be curled up with hunger pains before our volleyball game that night.

The rest of the day continued in a haze, my mood lifting only so slightly in band class, where I fully enjoyed playing first-chair clarinet. When the final bell rang, my stomach called out to me, clearly upset that I didn't eat my lunch. "Oh, shush," I scolded my belly, which earned me a few odd stares.

I shoved my notebook in my locker and took several deep breaths. I needed to calm down if I was going to do well at the game tonight. Our JV team hadn't lost all season, and there was only a week of games left. I wasn't about to lose one because of a bad day, which wasn't honestly all that bad anyway. Gosh, what was up with me?

"Ready?" Emma said cheerfully as we walked toward the locker room to gather our equipment.

"Ready as I'll ever be, I guess." I gave her a smile in hopes that it would cheer me up.

CHAPTER 3

*W*hen we got on the bus, I quickly claimed one of the empty seats near the back and placed my book bag on my lap. Emma sat next to me the same time Derek popped his head up over the seats at the front of the bus as he climbed the stairs.

"There are my two favorite girls." He smiled, taking the seat in front of us. "Chin up, Crystal."

I knew he was trying to get me to smile, but the way he touched my chin as he said this simply annoyed me further.

"Knees and nose," I said, pointing to the front of the bus while repeating the phrase the teachers used to tell us in elementary school. "Knees and nose to the front," they'd tell us for safety reasons.

Derek backed away from me with his eyebrows raised. "Someone woke up on the wrong side of the bed."

I glared at him in warning. I loved Derek like a brother, but I wasn't in the mood for his bubbly attitude. "Yeah," I snapped.

He held his hands up in surrender. He turned away from

me and pointed his knees and nose to the front. "Well, it's obviously *someone's* time of the month," he muttered, intentionally saying it loud enough for me to hear.

I rolled my eyes while silently thinking to myself that I *wish* it'd be my time so that I could finally grow into my body.

"Are you okay?" Emma said when we were on the road traveling over the flat terrain of southern Minnesota.

I tore my gaze from the window to look at her. "Yeah. I just... I don't know. I feel weird. I just woke up in a bad mood, and it's been following me around all day."

"I know what you mean." She rolled her eyes. "Talk about being a teenage girl."

Derek popped his head back up over the seat. "And what exactly is that like?"

"Knees and nose," Emma scolded. I laughed as they teased each other, and they joined along in my giggles.

"Maybe I just need a girl's night," I said once our conversation was private again.

"Sure. Tomorrow night?"

"Yeah. It's your turn to host, Emma."

Emma crinkled her nose, which made her look more like a chipmunk than normal. She ran a hand through her dark curls. "My house? Are you sure? I mean, Andrea is way cooler than my parents."

"My mom's great, but I really like your house. You have way more fun things to do. Can we please stay at your house?"

She seemed reluctant, but she finally agreed.

It didn't take long to reach our opposing team's school. Coach Amy must have not noticed my bad mood because she put me in during the first set.

This was certainly not a good day. I bent my knees, ready

as the serves came over the net, but I felt so disoriented that I couldn't seem to hit the ball just right. I knew where the ball was going to go before it got there, but my motor skills took a nose dive.

My first serve slammed into the net, and when I tried bumping the ball over on the third hit, the net caught it again. To avoid this the next time, I sent the ball to the other side of the court with a set, but one of the girls on the opposing team spiked it. The ball soared past me before I could process what was going on. A whistle blew, and I knew Coach was rotating me out before she stood from the bench. I slumped over to the boundary line and gave Jenna a high-five as she took my spot.

"What's up, Crystal?" Coach Amy asked as I returned to the bench. "You're not at the top of your game like normal."

"Yeah, maybe I should just sit this one out."

And I did. Coach didn't put me back in for the second or third set, either. I was so out of it that I hadn't noticed when the game was over. When I looked up, all I saw were the disappointed looks on my teammates' faces. I didn't have to look at the scoreboard to know we lost our first match of the season. My shoulders slumped in disappointment to meet the expressions of my teammates.

Coach called us together before we left the court. "I don't want you girls to get too disappointed over this. You've done great this season. You played well tonight, but we can do better next week. Let's keep this as our only loss this year, okay? Team Hornets on one, two, three."

I kept to myself on the bleachers as the Varsity team warmed up. Emma was throwing serves over the net with them, and Derek was catching balls, so I didn't have my best friends to talk to. My eyes fixed on the girls warming up, but

I didn't fully process the picture until I saw a blonde ponytail swishing around on our side of the net.

I know that ponytail. It shouldn't be there.

As the girl with the ponytail turned, her brown eyes locked on mine. The other players were moving so fast that in an instant, the girl with the blonde ponytail disappeared.

I felt woozy as a shiver ran down my spine. My heart was beating so hard as if it might escape from my chest, and for a few moments, the sounds in the room ceased to exist. I bent my head down and rested my elbows on my knees, taking in slow, controlled breaths.

Finally, I regained my composure. The sounds of the gymnasium began to come back to life. I looked around uselessly, thinking for a moment that I would find an explanation somewhere in the gym.

But there was nothing. In that moment, I knew I had seen Olivia Owen for the second time that day.

No, I rationalized. *I didn't* see *her. I* imagined *her.* I watched the girls more closely and wondered if I mistook one of the other team members for Olivia, but no one looked remotely like her. Once my heart beat settled, I shook off the bogus idea. *Maybe I* am *going crazy*, I thought to myself.

Time flew by, and before I knew it, our side of the gym erupted into cheers for the Varsity's win.

The bus ride home wasn't exciting since most of the people fell asleep. After working on a few homework problems under the light of my cell phone, I nodded off with them. When we arrived at the school, I deposited my equipment in my gym locker and changed back into my normal clothes.

"See you girls tomorrow," Derek promised when we came out of the locker room.

"Bye, Derek," Emma and I said together. Emma smiled

back at him, and I couldn't help but notice that she batted her eyes a bit when she did it. We walked most of the way home together but took our separate ways at our normal corner. I wondered briefly if I should tell Emma I was getting sick, but I didn't want to worry her.

"See you tomorrow morning," Emma waved. "And don't be late."

"I won't. I promise." I actually cracked a smile at that.

When I walked through the door, the smell of brownies hit my nose. I dropped my backpack instantly and raced into the kitchen. There on the counter sat a scrumptious-looking pan of freshly baked brownies. Well, they looked good if you could get past the crusty edges, which I was okay with at the moment. Without bothering to say hello to my mother, I dug in. Sweet, delicious chocolate after a day so sour felt great.

"Hungry?" my mom teased.

She was more like a friend to me than a mother.

"I had an awful day. Back off." I narrowed my eyes at her, a warning that I might bite her hand off if she touched my brownies. It was a lighthearted glare, and she knew it. Even I couldn't hide the smile twitching at the sides of my mouth.

"How did the game go?"

"We lost."

I felt bad that my mom couldn't be there for my games, but she had a business to run, and with Halloween just around the corner, it was the busiest time of the year for her. Mom owned a small shop on Main Street called Divination that specialized in everything Halloween, from costumes and decorations to candy and crystal balls. She and her two friends, Sophie and Diane, kept the business going by selling homemade candy and supernatural products like tarot cards throughout the year.

My mother let out a long yawn. "Well, I'm going to bed. I

just wanted to make sure you made it home safe. And, you know, I had to make you brownies. I had a feeling you'd need them tonight."

My mom was always so considerate and somehow knew exactly what I needed when I needed it. Right now, double chocolate brownies were my solace.

"Mom," I said. "Can I stay over at Emma's tomorrow night after practice?" I knew I didn't have to ask, but I did anyway to be courteous.

"Sure."

Once my mom left the kitchen and I felt like I'd eaten enough brownies, I covered the pan and went to get ready for bed. I flipped on the light in the bathroom and brushed my teeth. When I sat on the toilet, I thought I was imagining things.

Nope. My underwear was clearly stained. I had finally started my period!

So that's what my bad mood was all about, I thought. *If that's what PMS is, I'm not sure I want to be a woman anymore,* I joked with myself.

I searched under the sink for something to help me with my issue and found a half-empty package of pads. Soon afterwards, I crawled into bed and fell asleep.

CHAPTER 4

I woke with a start. My legs were tangled around my sheets, my whole body was wet with sweat, and my heart was pounding hard against my chest. I knew I had woken from a nightmare, but the details of the dream now eluded me as I struggled to remember what had terrified me.

I lay in bed for several long minutes until an image of my nightmare resurfaced in my mind. I remembered the sound of a car door shutting. I recalled the way the interior light lit up my face in the side mirror. No, not my face. It was the face of a young girl—maybe six—with brown hair and big chocolate eyes full of terror. As quick as I saw the image in my mind, it was gone.

When I finally calmed down, I made sure to fully dress before leaving my room because I could smell eggs and bacon. That only meant one thing: Teddy was here. The first time my mom's boyfriend came over in the morning to make breakfast for us, I made the mistake of coming out of my bedroom in just a t-shirt and undies. I really should have made the connection that there wasn't the smell of charred breakfast in the air, which meant someone other than my mother was cooking. Needless to say, it was a bit embarrassing.

When I entered the kitchen, I gave Teddy a hug. I was glad he was cooking since my mother was known to burn food and I had the tendency to over salt everything. I was fine with just a bagel, but I could take bacon and eggs any day.

Teddy and I got along well. Mom had been dating him for a few years, but he hadn't filled that hole in my chest where my father belonged. I was sure he never would, but I still liked him.

An image of the crash replayed in my head as I thought about my father. It wasn't a memory of the real car crash since I wasn't there, but rather a memory of a dream I had before it happened. It was strange that I dreamt that my father died in a car accident and then he did. Young children do have wild imaginations.

"Yum," I smacked my lips. "Bacon and eggs."

I reached into the cupboard and pulled out three plates and set them on the table.

"Almost ready, Kiddo."

Normally I would hate if people called me kiddo, but I really didn't mind when Teddy did as long as he let me to call him Teddy Bear whenever I wanted as a way to embarrass him. He didn't mind, even when he brought me to the police station once to show me around and I'd called him Teddy Bear in front of his coworkers. They just laughed, but he managed to laugh along, too.

"Mom!" I shouted down the hall. "Breakfast."

Teddy and I took our spots around the table. He didn't live with us, but he might as well have since he spent most of his time here when he wasn't at work.

My mother entered the room. The way Teddy gazed at her in awe told me he really did love her. In a flash, an image of a diamond ring popped into my mind, but it was gone before I could process it. *I hear wedding bells*, I thought silently.

"So how's everything going with planning for the festival?" Teddy asked my mother.

I was intrigued to know this, too, so I listened carefully.

"Most of our responsibilities are set up, but there's another meeting before the festival, and we still have to get a few things together for our booths."

My mom was talking about the booth she and her business partners set up at the Peyton Springs Halloween Festival every year. Since they're the experts in town on Halloween, they graciously volunteered. Plus, it was really good for business promotion.

Mom ran a fortune telling booth and dressed up as a gypsy every year. She knew all about the superstitions with tarot card readings and crystal balls, but it was, of course, all just for fun. A lot of people raved about how accurate she was, but that was just because she was so involved in the community that she knew everything about everyone. It was actually kind of funny to see people talk about how great she was when she was really just faking it, but I guess people wanted to believe in that kind of stuff around Halloween.

Sophie and Diane helped out with other things at the community festival like the haunted trail, carnival games, and other fun things.

"We have some really awesome ideas this year, and the

haunted trail is going to be better than ever before," my mother continued. "There are lots of people willing to help out, and Sheryl and Tammy are really doing a lot to make this year a blast."

Sheryl Stratton and Tammy Owen were the co-heads of the festival, but they were always begging my mom and her friends for help, which I found odd. My mom should have just taken over the festival. *But then again,* I thought, *maybe Tammy needs it this year to help her get past this difficult time.* After all, we had just passed the anniversary of her daughter's death, which left me feeling kind of bad for her. I applauded her for how she was holding together and getting so much done with the festival.

"I'll try to be there," Teddy said, "but I can't make any promises. We've had a lot of work at the station lately."

I crunched into my bacon. It was like heaven in my mouth. I moaned, causing my mom and Teddy to stare at me. "What?" I said innocently. "It's good."

The kitchen went silent again when we dug into our food. Teddy was the one to break the silence. "I was wondering if you girls are busy tomorrow night."

My mom and I exchanged a glance. "No," she answered. "What did you have in mind?"

Teddy shrugged, but it didn't feel like honest nonchalance to me. He seemed nervous about something. "I just wanted to take you girls out. We haven't gone out in a while."

"Is it a special occasion?" I asked.

"No. I just thought it would be fun."

My mom looked at me again and nodded lightly. "Sounds great."

I left the house in a much better mood than the day before and made it to the corner the same time Emma approached. "Looking better," she complimented.

"Feeling better," I agreed.

As we strolled to school, I was reminded of the scene we walked into yesterday with the fundraiser. I thought about Olivia briefly and wondered again if I should tell Emma that I thought I saw her in the hallway. I decided not to. It would just come across sounding as if I was crazy. When I told people in my kindergarten class that I had a friend named Eva, who apparently no one else could see or talk to, my classmates called me crazy. All it took was me telling Eva to go away before I made friends with Emma and passed the phase of imaginary friends. Maybe I could tell Olivia to go away and her face wouldn't appear in my mind. *That is, if I ever see her again, and since I'm not crazy,* I told myself, *I don't believe that I will.* I didn't say anything to Emma.

I had a much more successful day at practice, killing my serves and reacting quickly.

When practice ended, I was about ready to eat a horse. I mentioned this to Emma. "Ugh, I want food *now,* but I still have to go home and get my stuff for overnight."

"Why don't you go get your stuff, and I'll go home and start the pizza," she offered. "It should be ready when you get there."

"Deal," I agreed.

Emma and I walked to our corner. In our privacy, I again considered telling her about what happened to me. I still wasn't sure about talking about Olivia. *But I should at least tell Emma about getting my period, right?* I thought. *Perhaps that's something best saved for girl talk tonight, or maybe that's too private to mention.* I tried thinking back to when Emma started her period. I couldn't remember if she'd told me right away or not. The thought of what I should and shouldn't say still nagged at me as we went our separate ways toward our homes.

When I entered the door to our one-story house, Diane and Sophie sat in our living room.

"Girls night for you, too?" I asked before they had a chance to greet me.

"Yep," Sophie answered as she bounced up from the couch. She held me at arm's length. "Is something bothering you, sweetie?"

"Does being a teenage girl count as an excuse?"

Diane laughed from her spot on the couch. "Sure it does."

Sophie embraced me, which helped soothe me. I wrapped my arms around her small frame. Sophie was about my height with curly brown hair and bright eyes. She always seemed upbeat and happy.

Diane, on the other hand, was completely her opposite, which helped balance them out as best friends. Diane was a bigger woman with long, thick auburn hair that she always piled on top her head. She was less laid back and more serious.

"It's great to see you guys, but I have to pack up my stuff and head over to Emma's."

I went to my room and filled a bag with overnight supplies.

"Do you want a ride, Crystal?" my mom shouted from the kitchen when I reentered the main room.

"No, Mom. I'll walk."

She poked her head around the wall separating the two rooms. "Are you sure? It's getting dark."

"Mom, it's only a few blocks. I'll be fine."

"Okay, sweetheart. I'll see you tomorrow."

"Bye, Mom. Catch you later, girls."

It really wasn't a long walk to Emma's house, but I found myself second-guessing if I had packed everything I needed.

I mentally ticked off all the necessities in my head. As if the cramps in my abdomen were trying to tell me something, I knew immediately what I had forgotten. Even though I was nearly to Emma's, I turned back toward my house.

CHAPTER 5

hen I arrived back home, Sophie's car was
gone. *They must have gone to the shop to play
cards*, I thought. I never understood why they went there
instead of playing at our kitchen table. There was plenty of
room. I didn't fret on it too much.

I knew it wouldn't take me long to get what I came for,
but when I looked under the sink in the bathroom, I found
nothing but an empty package. I must have taken the last pad
this morning without realizing it, and I had used the last one
in my backpack for volleyball practice.

I stood from the sink wondering what I was going to do. I
could ask Emma, but that seemed almost embarrassing, and I
didn't want to just take her pads without asking. Plus, I knew
Emma used tampons, and I was *not* ready for that. Weren't
they uncomfortable?

I headed to the hall closet where we kept linens and extra
bath supplies, but no matter how far back I dug, there
weren't any feminine products around.

The gas station wasn't far. Maybe I could go pick some up. That plan seemed like a good idea until I remembered that I didn't have any cash. Maybe Mom had some stashed away, but I was not the kind of girl who would steal money from her mother's purse. Besides, my mom probably had her purse with her.

That left only one option. I would have to go to the shop and ask my mom for a few dollars. She'd have to find out eventually that I'd started my period. I might as well tell her sooner than later.

The shop wasn't far from our house. It was only three blocks down to Main Street and then a few more in the direction toward Emma's house. The gas station was on the corner. It would hardly take me out of the way.

When I arrived at Divination, I wasn't entirely sure my mother was there. The lights were turned off, and it seemed quiet. When I cupped my hands around my eyes and pressed my face to the front window's glass, though, I could see a faint light creeping out from one of the doors in the back.

I headed around to the back of the building and tried the door. Sure enough, it let me in freely as if it was willing me to join their girl's night. When I stepped into the hallway, I didn't hear the giggles and commotion that I expected from my mother and her two best friends. Normally they'd be loudly bickering and accusing each other of bluffing while laughing hysterically, yet those weren't the sounds I heard coming at me down the hall.

Instead, I heard a quiet humming noise that I couldn't place and smelled the faint scent of a familiar aroma. I guessed it was incense or a candle of some kind, but I didn't know exactly what scent they'd lit. A sense of eeriness overcame me, and I was suddenly afraid of what I might find. I neared the door with the light shining around the corners. It caught me off guard for a moment.

They wouldn't be in there, would they? I thought. *That's the storage room, not the break room. Or am I wrong? What if they left the door unlocked by mistake and someone is robbing their storage room?*

My heart raced as I considered this possibility. A shiver ran down my spine, and I felt a shift in the air. Still, my body sweated nervously. I considered turning around and fleeing for a moment, but I was too curious to turn away.

What would I do if there was someone else here, though? I would scream, I decided. *I would scream and run as fast as I can.*

My heart pounded on the walls of my chest, reverberating through my ears as I neared the door. I began to feel faint. I grabbed the handle with my damp palms and twisted slowly, and then in one quick motion, I whipped the door open.

My heart beat slowed when I found nothing in the storage room but a bunch of boxes. I switched off the light and let the door fall shut with a click.

Once I was back in the dark hallway by myself and ready to leave, the humming noise caught my attention once again. What was that? I followed the sound and pressed my ear against the door that led to the break room.

I could hear muffled voices, but I didn't see a light under the door. Who was in there? The sound, I realized, was a woman humming a stagnant note.

"We're here to help you," Sophie's voice rang over the humming.

I didn't take a moment to consider what they were doing behind the door. Once I was sure it was my mother and her friends, I wasn't scared anymore.

I had only a split second to take in the scene. The three girls sat in a circle around the break table, their hands connected as if in prayer. Candles lit up their faces. Just beyond the table stood another girl with blonde hair and brown eyes. Olivia Owen's ghost stared back at me with that same look of urgency.

"Help," she mouthed, but I didn't hear any sound come out.

The sight of Olivia lasted only a moment before the women jerked their eyes up at me in surprise and pulled their hands back, breaking their circle. Olivia disappeared.

My jaw dropped. *What is this? What are they doing?*

"Olivia," I murmured before I could stop myself, although I wasn't sure they could hear me. My racing heart returned, and my fingers quivered against the door knob. I felt hot and sweaty all over at the same time a chill overcame me. I was frozen in place and holding my breath.

I am crazy, I thought.

My mother smiled at me innocently like I hadn't just walked in on some satanic ritual. "Can I help you with something, sweetie?"

I couldn't find my mouth to formulate my words. I stayed where I was, unmoving for several long seconds as my eyes fixed on the empty space where Olivia stood only moments ago. When I regained my composure, I simply spat out, "I need some cash."

My mother rose from the table, grabbed her purse off the hook near the door, and led me out into the hallway. "It'll just be a minute," she assured her friends as she guided me out of the room.

My whole body trembled and felt weak as I tried to make sense of what I had just seen. I knew what I had seen, and I couldn't deny the fact any longer. I *was* crazy. Olivia's ghost?

What was Olivia doing in my mother's shop? Could my mother see her? Did I imagine her?

"Wh—What? Did I—? Were you—?" I spattered, unable to put my thoughts into words. Did they know Olivia was there? I couldn't quite understand what had frightened me so much. Was it the fact that I saw Olivia? Was it the fact that I knew for sure that I had seen Olivia at school the previous day? Or was it because I started believing that I was going crazy?

"We were just meditating," my mother said.

"Meditating," I said without inflection, still trying to catch my breath.

"It helps relieve stress."

Really, meditating? Because to me it looked like you were conducting a séance. But this kind of stuff is just for kicks! It isn't real, right? I tried to rationalize.

"I just need some money for pads," I managed to say almost normally.

My mother smiled at me as if relieved. She reached into her purse and pulled out her wallet. "Here you go. This should be enough."

I grabbed the bill and thanked her before I turned my back and headed toward the door.

"Have a good night, sweetie." She disappeared back into the break room.

When I reached the back door, I paused for a moment and crept back to the break room. I pressed my ear against the door to listen.

"I don't know what she thought," my mother said. "I mean, she can't know what's going on, right? Then again, she just started her period. Maybe there is still hope for her."

Hope? Hope that I'd finally grow into my breasts and my hips. If only.

The gas station sat another block down, and when I went in, I used the extra money I had left over to buy a bag of chips. I knew I'd be late to Emma's. I was hoping this would be enough of an apology. I picked out her favorite, Old Dutch dill pickle chips, even though I didn't really like the flavor.

When I got to her house, I knew she was about to scold me for being late. I lifted up the bag of chips, and that was enough to make her squeal in excitement.

"I totally forgive you for letting the pizza go cold."

I smiled back at her, and within minutes, my bad mood from the previous day and fright of what I'd seen earlier melted away. I felt completely comfortable at Emma's. Once we started gorging on pizza, soda, and chips, I was back to my normal self.

"Where's your dad?" I asked, half expecting Emma's father to come around the corner and make a silly joke like normal. Her mother was sitting at the kitchen table going over some paperwork and ignoring us. Her younger sister Kate was in the living room, but their family didn't feel complete without John there.

"He's not here," Emma answered as if I was supposed to know where he was.

Oh, well, I thought.

We spent the rest of the night tackling homework and goofing off in Emma's room while ignoring Kate's pleas to play with us.

"We don't *play*," Emma insisted.

When we sent Kate to watch a movie in the living room, she fell asleep almost instantly, leaving us alone upstairs to read magazines, listen to music, and try out different makeup techniques. Emma was great with makeup whereas I had a difficult time putting on eyeliner.

I was trying, and failing miserably, to put on a dark line across my eye when Emma turned off the radio.

"What was wrong with that song? I liked it."

Emma wrinkled her nose. "I hate that song. Let's listen to some real music." She sifted through her stacks of CDs to find one she liked. "Crap. I can't find the one I want. That was my favorite CD! Oh, well. We'll listen to this one instead. You can pick something if you want."

I sighed, finally giving up on my eyeliner. Emma returned to the mirror and began powdering her dark complexion. I switched spots with her and shuffled through her CDs. Where I collected owl décor, Emma collected CDs. I recognized several that I'd given her from birthdays and Christmases in the past as I ran my hands across the cases and read the artists' names. Suddenly, an idea struck.

I stood up almost too quickly and fell back down at her open closet.

She turned to look at me in confusion. "What are you doing?"

I didn't know how I knew, but I knew where she had lost her favorite CD. I threw clothes out of the way that she had let lay on her closet floor—the only part of her room that wasn't pristine—and flung myself deeper into her closet. I couldn't see what I was doing, but sure enough, my hand finally fell around the corners of a CD case. I pulled it out and looked at it in triumph.

"Is this the CD you're looking for?" I asked, holding it out to her.

"Oh, my gosh!" she squealed. "Yes! I don't know how it got in there. Thank you."

We ended the night by watching scary movies and

falling asleep in her queen-sized bed around four in the morning. I woke up around 10:00 a.m. and checked my phone for messages. There was a text from my mom telling me to be home by noon because I had chores to do. After chocolate chip pancakes, I said goodbye to Emma and headed home.

"Thanks for staying the night," she said. "I don't know what I'd do Friday nights without you."

As I neared my house, the memory of the previous night at the shop came flooding back to the forefront of my mind. Did I really see Olivia in my mom's shop? How was that possible?

I contemplated telling my mother about what I had seen in case I needed help or something. What if I started seeing other people, like my dad? I was sure that would make me go crazy for real, and I needed someone there to support me when they put on the straight jacket.

When I entered the house, my mom was already preparing lunch.

"I'm not hungry," I told her.

"That's fine because I didn't make you any food. I figured you would have eaten already."

I watched my mother set her grilled cheese sandwich on the table. It was charred in the middle. How had she not learned how to cook yet? She paced back around the counter and pulled one of the glasses from the drying rack.

Should I tell her? I wondered. My hands shook and my stomach knotted as I tried to work up the courage to say anything.

"Mom," I managed.

"Yeah?" she said as she turned from the sink and took a sip of water from her glass.

I paused for a moment, unsure if I should admit I was

going crazy, but in the next second, I knew I had to say it. I spat it out before I could stop myself.

"I saw Olivia Owen last night."

My mother's eyes widened, her jaw dropped, and the glass in her hand fell to the floor and shattered.

CHAPTER 6

"How could you hide something like this from me?" I stared at my mother in disbelief, trying to process what she'd just said. I wanted to be mad at her for keeping this a secret, but I just couldn't.

An expression of guilt fell over my mother's face. She sat across from me at the dining room table after we'd cleaned up the glass shards. She had just told me the truth about my heritage.

As much as some people would run from the house screaming that my mother was a crazy person, I believed every word she said. Perhaps it was exposure to the paranormal through her business, even if I always believed her crystal balls and tarot cards were fake. Whatever the reason, I wasn't terrified. It was comforting to know that I wasn't actually going crazy.

"I'm sorry. I didn't think you had the gift. I wanted you to live a normal life."

"What do you mean?"

"Crystal, you have to understand," my mother pleaded,

trying to justify her actions. She really didn't need to. I wasn't mad at her. I was just confused. "Being psychic is hard. People will hurt you. It's not all rainbows and butterflies."

"Hurt me? How?"

She took a deep breath. "They'll either think you can give them something you can't, or they'll shun you because you can do something they can't. Sweetie," my mother said urgently, grabbing my hands from across the table. "You can't tell anyone. You know that, right?"

"Why not?"

"Some of them will call you a witch. Others will take advantage of you," she continued.

"But Mom, you use your gift every year at the Halloween festival," I pointed out. It was odd to think that all the fun she was having didn't originate from the town gossip but rather from her honest-to-god gifts.

Mom averted her gaze from my eyes and curled her mouth up guiltily. "Everyone thinks that's just for kicks. Even you didn't believe I could do it for real."

She was right. No one really believed she was a fortune teller. She played her role well, a woman who wasn't psychic but pretended to be. Except that she really was.

"What I'm saying," she continued, "is that you have to be careful. I'm carefully hiding out in the open where no one will notice."

I found that a bit ironic, but she was right. "Okay," I agreed. "I'll be careful, but can I at least tell Emma?"

My mother sighed. "I would advise against it. It's your own choice, but you have to be prepared for the consequences. You have to make sure she doesn't spread it around. I don't want people to hurt you." My mother's eyes brimmed with tears.

It took me a few seconds to realize the meaning behind her words. If I told anyone, it would put her secret at risk, too. Still, she was giving me that choice, which is something I really respected and appreciated.

"Mom, Emma's not like that."

"I know. I'm so sorry I didn't tell you, but you understand, right?"

I smiled. "Yeah, I understand, but how come you didn't think I had the gift? Did I not show any psychic tendencies?"

I could see it in my mother's eyes that she was looking into the past. "Do you remember your imaginary friend, Eva?"

"Of course I remember her."

"When you first mentioned her, I was happy and devastated at the same time. At one level, I wanted to share so much with you about the gift, but on another, I wanted you to live a normal life away from the supernatural. When I asked you if Eva was real, you said she wasn't and that you made her up. I assumed that she really was a figment of your imagination. It's not uncommon for children, especially those without siblings, to create imaginary friends at that age."

My mouth fell open in disbelief. I remembered the moment she was talking about. I had been in my room having a tea party with Eva when my mother knocked on my door.

"Who are you talking to, sweetheart?" she'd asked.

"Eva," I said in my high four-year-old voice.

My mother bent down beside my chair. "Sweetheart, who's Eva?"

"Eva's my friend."

"Where is Eva?"

"Right there." I pointed to the chair across from me. I

knew by my mother's expression that she didn't see Eva, my first friend my own age.

In fact, I knew that no one else could see Eva because none of the other kids at daycare could. When I had asked my babysitter if she could save a seat for Eva at lunch, she had a long talk with me about how Eva wasn't real and that I was imagining her. She told me that it wasn't healthy to have imaginary friends and that I should play with other kids at daycare. So when my mother looked me straight in the eyes and asked me if I believed Eva was real, I put on my best lying face and told her no, I had made Eva up. It was the only time I can remember blatantly lying to her.

"I told you she wasn't real because I thought I would get in trouble if I believed it," I told my mother.

She smiled at me across the dinner table. Then my mother erupted into laughter. I simply stared at her for a moment, unsure of what was so funny. When she didn't stop, I joined in the laughter.

"After that," my mother admitted, "you never really gave me a reason to believe you had a gift. I almost thought you were psychic when you guessed your birthday presents before you opened them. Remember that on your eighth birthday? You were so accurate, but then I figured you peeked before I had a chance to wrap them. I didn't want to ruin your fun, so I didn't say anything."

I hadn't ever peeked.

"There were other times when I thought… maybe… but I convinced myself that I was *looking* for reasons to tell you about my—our—gift."

Memories flooded back into my mind, and suddenly, so much more about my life made sense. "I guess I must have hid a lot from you."

"Like what?"

I picked at my fingernails and kept my head low.

"Like what?" she prodded.

"You know when Dad died?"

"You saw his ghost?" she squealed in shock.

I was taken aback by this statement because it never occurred to me that my father roamed the world as a ghost. "A ghost? No. Is that what Eva was? A ghost?"

My mother stared into the distance for a moment. "Most likely. She could have been your spirit guide, but I'm guessing she was just a lonely girl who needed someone to play with."

"My spirit guide?"

"Everyone has one. They're like angels who guide you in the choices you make in life. I speak to my spirit guide all the time."

My spirit guide? I may have had psychic visions in the past, but I'd never spoken with a spirit guide.

"What happened with Dad?" my mother asked.

"Well, before he died," I started reluctantly, "I dreamt of the accident before you ever told me about it."

My mother gasped. "You—you saw your father die before it happened?"

"Yeah. I think so. I mean, I always thought it was just a coincidence. Do you think it was a vision?"

My mother's lips pressed together deep in thought. I gave her a moment to digest this.

Her next words came out as a whisper. "Do you know what this means?"

"No," I whispered back. Where was she going with this?

"Crystal, there are different types of psychics. Some can predict the future. Others can see the past. Some psychics see ghosts while others hear voices. Do you see where I'm going with this?"

"No," I admitted.

"Crystal, most people don't see spirits *and* predict the future. I mean, we can communicate with them—it's easier in numbers, and that's why séances work—but rarely do people like me *see* them. You clearly have an amazing ability. More amazing than any of us could have predicted. What else should I know?"

I thought for a moment. "That's pretty much it. I can usually tell who's calling before I check caller I.D., but I always wrote that off as luck. Besides, you don't need to be psychic to know who's calling these days."

My mother smiled at this.

I continued. "I always know when it's going to rain, but I took that as a sign that I would make a great meteorologist."

My mom laughed. "Anything else?"

I froze. I knew she would believe me, but saying it out loud made me feel like I'd have to admit it was real. But it was, wasn't it? I took a deep breath. "I've seen Olivia Owen's ghost three times now."

My mother didn't call me crazy, and she wasn't about to contact the mental institution, either. "Three times?"

"Yeah. I saw her at school Thursday morning, at the volleyball game, and in the break room last night."

"You saw her last night." It wasn't a question, only a statement to mull the idea over.

"Yeah, when I went to go get money from you," I clarified even though I didn't need to.

"Are you sure?"

"Yes." Why was she grilling me? "Why?"

She closed her eyes to soothe herself. "We've been trying to contact Olivia for weeks, but we couldn't get through to her."

Why was my mother trying to contact Olivia? "Is Olivia in trouble?"

"Maybe," my mom started, but she was cut off by the sound of the front door opening. Teddy was here already. "We'll talk later." Before Teddy came too far into the house, Mom added with a whisper, "Teddy doesn't know."

Teddy entered the kitchen and looked from me to my mother and back again, and we shot him stares of our own. He held his hands up in defense. "Whatever girl talk stuff is going on here, I don't care to know."

CHAPTER 7

*N*ow that Teddy was here, Mom and I couldn't continue our conversation in case he overheard. It was only about one o'clock, so we had plenty of time to kill before he took us out to dinner. When I walked into my bedroom, I understood completely why my mother wanted me home early. I really did need to do some chores and clean my room.

My bedroom was my place of solace. The walls were white since I'd painted over the pale yellow a few years ago. I'd added a wall decal beside my bed of two colorful owls sitting on a branch together. There was other owl décor spread throughout the room. And it was utterly a mess. Clothes, both clean and dirty, were strewn around along with pieces of homework, books, and other crap I hadn't realized I'd even used recently.

I started with my stuffed animal owl collection in the corner, straightening their wings and setting them upright on their shelves. I took special care of the gray one I called Luna, the one my father had given me that had started the collection. I set her next to the larger black one I'd named David after my father.

My collection brought me back to the memory of my father's death. He used to be a math teacher at the middle school. That night was parent teacher conferences, which meant he was working late. Perhaps if he wasn't out so late, he wouldn't have been hit by a drunk driver. I doubted my father even saw him coming before the full-sized pick-up truck hit him head-on.

Maybe if I'd said something about my dream, we could have warned him. The thought only wounded my heart further. I knew there was nothing I could do to change what had happened nearly a decade ago.

I forced down the lump in my throat. When all of my owls were in order, I turned back to the rest of my room and prepared myself to tackle it.

I slowly organized piles of clothes and other random belongings and then walked down to the basement to do my laundry, all the while trying to sort through the overwhelming information I'd just stumbled upon.

I was psychic? I was really psychic? How powerful were my abilities? What could I do? What would Emma say when she found out? How would I tell her? Would I tell her? Why was it so easy for me to believe in this nonsense? Was it nonsense?

So many questions raced through my head. I let my clothes sit next to me in the basket as I took a seat on top of the dryer. I folded my legs and rested my hands on my knees. I closed my eyes and took in a deep breath.

How do I use my abilities? I tried focusing on my breathing to relax myself, but it didn't work. I thought maybe if I focused, I would be able to see something, maybe even see Olivia again to find out what she needed, but nothing came. There was still too much confusion clouding my mind.

What good is being psychic if I can't see things at will? I thought as I hopped down, annoyed, and threw my clothes in the washer, not bothering to separate the whites from the colors.

When I went back up to my room, I suddenly lost all forms of motivation I'd had from earlier. Although my room was only half clean, I fell down on my bed, intending to sort out the thoughts in my mind.

Moments later, my mother was knocking at my door. She peeked her head into my room and frowned at the mess, but she didn't say anything about it.

"Crystal, it's time to get ready to go."

Go? Go where?

I glanced at the clock on my nightstand. Holy crap, I'd fallen asleep for nearly three hours. Where had the time gone?

"Teddy wants you to dress nice."

My mother closed my door quietly, and I got ready to go out. I put on a sun dress with blue flowers, which seemed to be the nicest thing in my closet. I let my hair fall down around my body and slipped on a pair of fancy sandals. I applied mascara as a final touch.

"Don't you have anything nicer to wear?" Teddy asked when he saw me.

I looked down at my dress. I thought it looked fine. "Nicer?"

He laughed. "I'm just kidding, Kiddo. I think you look great."

My mother came out a few minutes later looking as gorgeous as ever in a blue halter dress that showed off her slim figure. She had twisted her hair up and applied some makeup. I could tell she hated it. "Why so fancy?"

Teddy rose from his chair and held out his elbow for her.

He was wearing sleek black pants, a button down shirt, and a tie.

Why is he doing this? I wondered. *He said this wasn't a special occasion.* Before I could finish the thought, I knew exactly what the special occasion was.

∾

Teddy didn't bother telling us where we were going, but it didn't surprise me when we reached the city and stopped outside of Amant. My mother clearly had no idea what was going on as Teddy led her through the front doors.

"Why so fancy?" she asked again.

Please, Mom, I thought. *If you're psychic, how can you not see what's happening?*

Teddy shrugged. "I just thought we could use a nice meal." He gave my mother a peck on the lips before turning to talk with the host about our reservations. I got the impression that Teddy had this planned for quite some time but was still trying desperately to keep things casual. It wasn't working so well for him.

The host led us through the restaurant to an elegant table set with a romantic blossom centerpiece. We took our seats and ordered drinks before searching over the menu. How could my mother not see what was going on, especially with these prices? Steak and fries for $30? *It better be a pretty good steak,* I thought.

I decided to order salmon the same time our drinks arrived, and I silently sipped on my lemon water while Mom and Teddy chatted about the menu.

"I was thinking about getting the lobster," my mother announced.

"I was thinking the same thing. Maybe I should order something else, and we could share," Teddy offered.

My mother gazed up at him and smiled. They ogled at each other from across the table for what seemed like forever before finally deciding on what to order. I tried not to blush at their obvious flirting.

We ordered our dinner and talked about trivial matters while we waited. Teddy was a great guy, but he could get a bit dull at times, so I tuned him out. I let my mind wander, again exploring the implications of my abilities while trying to sort through all the questions I still had. I thought of Olivia again. What did she need help with?

When our food came, Teddy finally quieted. I sat in peace listening to the tranquil music in the background and savoring my delicious fish. I watched as Teddy and my mom shared food, actually feeding each other. My first instinct was to gag, but then I reminded myself why I was here. I smiled, wondering when the excitement of the night would climax. This was a memory I was sure I wanted to hold onto, so instead of letting my mind wander, I focused on the couple before me, so happy and in love.

As the food on our plates began to disappear, our mouths started moving more. When my mother asked about Teddy's parents in Florida, she set up his speech far too well, and he took advantage of this.

"I'm glad you asked because the last time I talked to them, they suggested that we all go down there for Thanksgiving, their treat."

Mom's face twisted as if she didn't know how to answer the question.

I thought it was a great idea. We didn't have family in the area. The only reason we lived in Peyton Springs was because my parents moved here to partner with Sophie and

Diane on their business. Sophie was the only one with family in the area out of the three of them. Teddy had family nearby, too, and I'd met most of them, but his parents retired to Florida and traveled the tropics most holidays. We still hadn't had a chance to meet them, so it only made sense to leave Minnesota on Thanksgiving weekend. Getting away from the chilly November weather and lying on the beach sounded fantastic to me.

"I—I guess we'd have to think about it." My mother shot me a nervous glance. "I'd love to meet your parents."

Teddy scratched his head. "The thing is, I don't want you to meet my parents for the first time and have to introduce you as my girlfriend and her daughter."

"What do you mean?" she asked.

Teddy shifted in his chair and reached inside his pocket.

"Your other one," I whispered, unsure of where that came from.

He shoved his hand in his other pocket and pulled out a small black box. He nodded toward me as a thank you gesture while he pulled his brows together in an expression that begged the question, *How did you know?*

"What I mean is that I'd rather introduce you as my future wife and future step-daughter." He hesitated for a moment before rising from his chair and bending down onto one knee beside my mother.

My mom's hands flew to her mouth, and her eyes widened in surprise. How did she *not* see this coming?

Teddy opened the box, and even under the soft glow of the restaurant lights, the familiar diamond I'd seen in my mind shined with every facet. Their eyes locked in a lover's stare.

"Andrea Mae Frost, will you do the great pleasure of being my wife?"

A small sound escaped my mother's lips, although I wasn't sure it was meant to be an answer.

Teddy raised a pointer finger to stop her and placed the box beside her on the table. He reached into his pants pocket again and pulled out another small box and turned to me. When Teddy opened the box, tears welled up in my eyes. Inside the box sat a gorgeous pendant of an owl, its body outlined in blue and black gems.

This was the most touching gesture. Now I understood how my mother didn't see the proposal coming. I had no idea Teddy was planning this for me, either.

"And Crystal Rhea Frost, I would be honored if you would give your mother and me your blessing and that you wouldn't mind if I became your step-father." He glanced toward my mom. "That is, if your mother says yes."

Was he trying to bribe me? Or was he saying that I was just as important to him as my mom was? I wasn't sure. All I knew is that my heart swooned at the gesture and that I loved Teddy enough to want him to marry my mother and hope she said yes.

My mother's eyes were still wide, but she let her hands fall to her lap. "Teddy, I—I." She glanced at me nervously. "I think we need to talk about this." She looked around at the crowd, who was beginning to stare, and then back at the ring. "I'm not saying no. I'm just saying it's a big step, and I think we should all talk about it privately."

Teddy rose from his place on the floor, his shoulders slumped as he sat back in his seat. "I completely understand," he said, although his fallen face told me this made him nervous.

"Let's just get the check," my mom insisted.

I reached toward the middle of the table where my beautiful necklace sat, box open, and snatched it up, closing it and placing it in my purse. I wanted to put it on immediately, but I couldn't predict how my mother would feel about that. If I could see the future, shouldn't I be able to tell?

"You have *my* blessing," I whispered, unsure if I had a place in the conversation.

I gave Teddy a sympathetic look when my mom wasn't watching, and he raised the corners of his mouth in reply. Neither of us had to be psychic to share a telepathic conversation.

Sorry about the way my mom answered, my expression said.

I was expecting a yes, but there's still a glimmer of hope, Teddy's eyes replied.

The car ride home was silent except for when Teddy asked if we could talk now.

"I'd like to speak to both of you separately," my mom answered.

When Teddy pulled into the driveway, he hesitated when getting out of the car. "Should I come in, too?"

My mom climbed out of the passenger seat and looked back at him. "Yes, please."

Teddy hung his head as if Mom was mad at him even though she clearly wasn't. I assured him of this when she was out of earshot, and he gave me another smile of thanks.

My mother left Teddy in the living room and led me into her bedroom to talk. When the door clicked behind her, she let her emotions run.

"I want to marry him so badly!" She danced about the room and plopped down on her bed. "Ugh, I don't know what to do."

I stared at her. My mom and I got along great, like best friends, but I'd never seen her act so much like a teenage girl.

"Why didn't you say yes, then?"

She stared back as if I just didn't get it. I really didn't

understand. If she wanted to marry him, why did she crush his spirits in the restaurant?

"It's not that simple, Crystal. In marriage, you shouldn't hide anything."

"Hide anything? What are you hiding?" I knew the answer before I finished the sentence. Teddy didn't know she was psychic.

"I love him so much, but before I can say yes, I need to make sure that he can live with my secret. I hate to put this responsibility on you, but I need you to help me figure out how to tell him."

CHAPTER 8

"*D*idn't you see this coming?" I asked. I wasn't referring to the fact that my mother was psychic. I was referring to the simple fact that she and Teddy were meant to be together. My dad died nearly 10 years ago. My mother and I were both ready to move on, and Teddy would make a great addition to our family.

"I may be psychic, Crystal, but I can't see everything."

"Why don't you just come out and say it?" I offered. "Just tell him about your ability, and if he can't deal, then tough luck. But Teddy loves you. He won't just *leave*."

My mother twisted her hands in her lap and fiddled with her purse strap. "I'm not sure he'll believe me. What if he thinks I'm playing some sick joke? What if he's scared of me?"

I didn't know how to answer my mother's questions. It was a lot to take in, and I wasn't used to my mother leaning on me like this. I wouldn't have believed her ability myself if I hadn't experienced it. Plus, I wasn't entirely sure what Teddy's take on religion was. I knew he didn't go to church, but if he wasn't open-minded about an afterlife, would he believe in the paranormal?

"Well, can't you just look into your crystal ball and figure out what to say?" I asked, half joking.

She twisted her face at me. "It doesn't work that way. I may be able to see the future, but I never get visions about my own future."

I moved across the room and sat next to her on the bed. "What if you could prove it by telling him something he doesn't know?"

"No," my mother whined. I gently rubbed her back to calm her. "I'm only partially clairvoyant. I only get feelings about the future. It's Diane who can see past events."

"What?" I practically squeaked. "Diane is psychic, too?"

"And Sophie," she said.

"But... how?"

My mom gave me a look that begged the question, *Really, you haven't figured it out yet?* She turned toward me and stared into my eyes intently. "How can I tell Teddy?"

"Well, I don't know the future, either!"

She looked at me seriously. "Crystal, I'm not asking your advice as a psychic. I'm asking your advice as a person, as my daughter. Normally I'd ask Sophie or Diane how to handle this, but I've learned that teenagers can have some pretty great insight, too."

She reached up and tucked a strand of hair behind my ear, and I suddenly understood. She was asking me because she wanted me to be part of the decision, of all of this. If she said yes, if she told him her secret, it wouldn't be just her secret she was telling him or her life she'd be affecting. Every move from here on out was sure to affect both of us.

I swallowed, stalling to come up with a good solution. "Mom, what does Teddy believe in?"

"What do you mean?"

"Like, does he believe in God?"

She cocked her head. "You know, of all the things I know about Teddy, this is one subject that we've never really talked about." She dropped her head guiltily. "I guess I always avoided it because I didn't want to reveal my secret."

"Mom, if you love him so much, why did you even hide it from him?"

Why did you hide it from me? I added in my head, but I didn't say it out loud.

"Crystal, you know your dad wasn't the only guy I dated, right?"

"Yeah," I said slowly, unsure where she was going with this.

"Well, I've told other boyfriends my secrets before, and you know what they did?" She didn't wait for an answer. "They left me, called me a witch. My high school boyfriend told everyone, and the bullying got so bad that I had to transfer schools."

My heart dropped. I didn't know my mother had ever been bullied. I was briefly reminded of kindergarten when my classmates called me crazy for having an imaginary friend, except I hadn't imagined her.

"I've always been careful about telling people since then, but your father still loved me after I told him, and he believed me." She blinked at me, holding back tears. "And now I hide behind the business and 'make believe' fortune telling just so that I can use my talents without telling anyone. It's so pathetic." She dropped her head, pulling her self-esteem along with it.

"No, Mom," I assured her as I reached out to rub her shoulder. "It's not pathetic."

"What if he doesn't believe me?" Her voice cracked.

"This is Teddy we're talking about. I think he'll love you no matter what you are. He loves you so much, he'd probably still marry you if he found out you were a dude."

My mom giggled and lifted her head to look at me. Her eyes sparked with tears that threatened to spill over her lids. "Maybe I just shouldn't say anything."

"Come on," I said, patting her shoulder. "I'll be there to help you, but you have to tell him. No more secrets, okay?" I hoped she knew I meant no more secrets from me, either.

"Okay."

"Now let's take a few deep breaths. Then we'll tell Teddy that we'd love him to be part of our family."

She smiled and wiped her nose as she let out a nervous giggle. "I'm sorry I dragged you into this. It's not a burden a mother should put on her child."

I continued rubbing her shoulder. "It's okay, Mom. It really is. I'll help you, okay? Let's go tell Teddy your secret." I paused. "Our secret," I corrected, which made my mom smile.

When we came back into the living room, Teddy was waiting patiently on the couch. He perked up as we entered. My mother hesitated, but I nudged her forward.

"T—Teddy," she started as she approached him hesitantly, and then she knelt down beside him and took his hands. "The reason I didn't say yes right away is because I can't go into a marriage having secrets."

They both glanced at me for a brief moment, my mother looking for encouragement and Teddy searching for some indication of what she was talking about.

"There's just something about me that you don't know, and if you can't accept it, I can't marry you."

Teddy squeezed her hand tighter. I watched from the corner, playing my role as observer. He stared into her eyes dreamily, speaking words of honesty. "Andrea, there's nothing you can say that would stop me from wanting to marry you."

That made my mother's lips twitch into a small smile. "It has to do with what I believe in. Teddy, what do you believe?"

He furrowed his brow. "You mean, do I believe in God?"

"Yes. What do you believe?"

He shifted. Perhaps the subject never came up because it was uncomfortable for him, too. "Well, I believe anything is possible."

I released the breath I didn't know I was holding. My mother did the same.

"Teddy," my mother addressed her soon-to-be fiancé but paused for a brief moment before continuing. "I believe there's another side out there. I believe there are spirits, family members waiting for us on the other side."

He gave her hand another tight squeeze. "Of course there are."

"I also believe that we can communicate with these spirits. Sometimes they tell us about the future. Sometimes they show us things we don't want to see. Sometimes they come to us for help."

Teddy nodded. "A lot of people believe in prophecies."

"Teddy," she said slowly. She paused for a moment, taking in a deep breath. "I believe I am one of those people."

She finally said it. The tension in my body waiting for this moment let go in quick release. I was proud of her. I only wished that when the time came, I would be able to muster up the same level of courage.

"One of what people?"

My mom shifted. "Someone who can communicate with spirits." She hesitated again. "Teddy, I'm... I'm a psychic."

Teddy looked from my mother, to me, then back to my mom. "You girls aren't joking with me, are you? I mean, I know you're into that supernatural stuff with the shop and the Halloween festival and everything, but you're serious?"

The tension in my body returned. He didn't believe her?

My mother dropped her head. I knew she was scared of what would happen next, but when she lifted her head to meet his gaze, she simply said, "Yes."

The next few moments stretched into an eternity, leaving me far too much time to think about the next possible outcomes. Would he storm off and call us crazy? Would he think we were still playing a joke on him? Would he hate us? The clock above the couch ticked, but it seemed too slow, each second pulsing in my ears, a thumping in my body. What would happen next?

Teddy stood and pulled my mother up from the floor. He placed a hand on each of her shoulders and looked her directly in the eye. "I can live with that," he said with a grin. He embraced my mother so hard, I could practically feel the hug in the air. My mother's face lit up, and she beamed at me. In a quick twitch of her head, she motioned for me to join them. I wrapped my arms around their bodies in a group hug.

When they finally pulled away from each other, my mother shouted, "Yes, yes, yes!" Teddy pulled the box from his pocket once again, knelt to the ground, and slipped the ring over her finger. "Yes!" she cried again as they embraced once more.

Once they settled their excitement, we all sat down, the happy couple cuddled on the couch while I sat on the matching chair. We talked about future plans, like when they would get married and where they would have the wedding.

I pulled the box Teddy had given me out of my purse and put on the necklace. It was the perfect length.

I still wasn't sure if Teddy believed us or not, but he at least seemed to accept that we believed it.

My mom suddenly pulled away from Teddy and looked him in the eyes. "Move in with us," she begged.

He smiled back at her. Without hesitation, he agreed.

It was nearly 11:30 when I started nodding off. They wanted me to be part of the planning stage, but I couldn't keep my eyes open anymore to process the plans they were making. My mother was going on about her dream cake when I excused myself. When I closed my door and finally had privacy in my room, I pulled out my phone and immediately texted Emma and Derek.

Mom and Teddy are getting married!!!

It wasn't even a minute later when I heard the familiar chimes notifying me of a text.

OMG!!! You woke me up, but that is AWESOME! Tell them congrats for me!

I was pleased by Emma's excitement and a little disappointed that Derek wasn't awake to send back a text. I felt like I'd been rude to him the other day, and I liked our texting conversations. Even so, I was really tired.

I wanted to tell Emma more about the big night and how it all went down, but I didn't know how to tell her without revealing my mother's, and now my, secret. I figured I'd tell her eventually, but I couldn't discuss something like this over text message. Plus, I was far too tired to stay awake texting, so I changed into my pajamas and fell asleep instead.

CHAPTER 9

I woke up to find Mom and Teddy at the breakfast table. I poured myself a bowl of cereal and joined them.

"Well, I have to take off," Teddy announced. He rose from the table and carried his dishes to the sink. "I have some paperwork at the station I need to get ready before the week starts. You girls have a good day."

My mother smiled up at him. She'd once told me that having a policeman as a boyfriend made her feel like she was dating a super hero.

Teddy's eyes fell on the owl necklace around my neck as he exited the room.

"You have a good day, too, Teddy Bear," I called after him.

When we were alone with our last few bites of breakfast, my mother spoke. "So, how are you holding up?"

"Holding up? I think your engagement is awesome. I love Teddy."

She set down her fork and looked at me across the table with a serious expression on her face. "That's not what I meant. I want to know how you're handling your abilities. Sometimes growing up can bring them out a bit."

What? Is she saying that I saw Olivia because I started my period? I had to admit, the events did seem to coincide.

"I think I'm fine," I answered. "It's just all so confusing."

"I know," she agreed, adding a sense of *I've been there before* to her tone. "It's just that we didn't get to finish our conversation, and I wanted you to be able to ask questions."

I thought about this for a moment. What *did* I want to know? Did I even want to be psychic, to have this burden over my head, this secret that I would have to hide from everyone, even from the people I loved the most? Did I want to go through what my mother went through? Maybe I could suppress my abilities. I had lived in Peyton Springs my whole life, but what if people found out? What would happen to Divination if the community discovered that the owners were really psychic? Would they drive us away or welcome us with open arms?

At the same time, I knew there had to be some good to come from it. If I could prevent a tragedy like my father's death by learning how to recognize my dreams as visions, then that was something I was willing to do.

As much as it confused me, I wanted to be psychic, to embrace the world beyond this one and to not run and hide from who I was. I met my mother's gaze again, knowing exactly what I wanted to ask.

"Will you teach me?"

Her face lit up.

~

Mom was talking too fast to process anything she was saying.

"Slow down," I begged as we neared Divination. Sophie was the one running the shop this weekend, but mom wanted to bring me in and teach me about the art of being psychic.

It was early on a Sunday morning, so there weren't a lot of people out shopping yet. When we entered Divination, there were two girls who I recognized from the middle school trying on costumes in the dressing room. Other than that, the shop was void of customers.

When the bell above the door rang, Sophie looked up from the costumes she was organizing. "What a surprise! Have you come to take over my shift?" she joked.

"No," my mom laughed as she gestured to Sophie to follow her toward the back. "Crystal, can you stay here just in case anyone comes in and needs help?"

I had worked at the shop in the past, but since I started high school, I rarely came in here.

My mom walked toward the break room while I took a seat on the stool behind the front counter. The shop looked a lot different than I remembered since it was Halloween. Any typically empty spaces on the walls were covered in fake cob webs, and the normal contents of the store were gone, replaced with rows of costumes.

I glanced around and focused on the girls trying on costumes.

"Oh, my gosh. Look at this amazing Roman costume," one of them raved from the dressing rooms toward my right.

"I hate this fairy costume. It's so itchy," the other one said. "I'm going to find a different one." She exited the dressing room and roamed the shop on her own. Clearly she didn't need my help.

Seeing as I wasn't needed, I rose from my chair and slipped around the counter. I ran my fingers across some of the costumes, but none of them stood out to me. I wanted to dress up for Halloween, but I was too old for trick-or-treating. A lot of people dressed up for the community festival. Maybe I could find a costume for that.

I flipped through the costumes on their hangers but found nothing interesting in that row, so I turned to the row behind me. From out of the corner of my eye, I noticed something sparkling from the next room. The building used to have several shops in it, so there was a wall separating the two main rooms with an open entryway between them. The other room was usually full of things like tarot cards, crystal balls, and magic kits.

As I peeked over the clothes rack, the sparkling caught my eye again as bright waves of light danced around the other room. *What is that?* I wondered. I was too intrigued to let it sparkle without investigating.

The young girls' laughter near the dressing room faded into nonexistence as I carried myself into the other room. The light glowed in my eyes, pulling me in. It played tunes of blissfulness and tranquility in my head. Without realizing it, I reached out and wrapped my hands around the source of the light. In my hands sat a glowing crystal ball. Its energy reached out to me and sent waves of happiness from my head to my toes. For a moment, it seemed as if the crystal ball and I were the only things in the world.

"Crystal," my mother called, pulling me from my trance. The other objects in the room returned to my vision, and the light emanating from the ball faded. All that was left in my hands was a regular crystal ball.

I turned around to see her standing in the doorway.

"Mom," I answered, dazed. "Can I get this?" I held out the crystal ball, showing her my new-found treasure.

"It's just a regular crystal ball." She inched into the room and headed over to the fancier balls they had on display, the ones with elegant bases or unique colors. "You don't want one of these more decorative ones?"

"I want this one," I told her, showing it to her once again as if it were a five-pound diamond. My next words came out as a whisper. "Mom, it speaks to me." I didn't think she heard me.

She waved her hand like she didn't care. "Sure, get whatever crystal ball you want."

I jumped in excitement and snatched up the base from the display. It was a simple stainless steel base with four legs. I exited the room and placed the ball on the front counter so I would remember it when we left. My mother followed behind me with a few products in her hands.

Sophie had returned and was again organizing costumes on their racks. I eyed her. Sophie was psychic, too? What kind of abilities did she have?

"What did you talk to Sophie about?" I followed my mother into the break room, which was a small room about the size of my bedroom with hooks and lockers against one wall and a counter against the other. In the middle of the room stood a square table with chairs placed around it.

"Well, I told her I was getting married. I also told her why we were here."

My mother set down the products in her arms on the break table and gestured for me to sit down. The first thing she grabbed was a deck of tarot cards.

I pushed myself away from the table. "Mom, I don't want to do this whole tarot card thing."

She already had the deck out of the box, and as soon as I said it, her face fell. Tarot card readings were her thing. I knew I'd hurt her the second I said it.

"It's just, you've tried showing me this stuff before," I

explained, remembering years ago when she tried to get me to help with the Halloween festival, "and I just don't like doing it. I want to learn more about *my* abilities. I don't think I'll ever be a tarot card reader."

She put down the deck as if she understood. "Okay, maybe we shouldn't start with this, then. How about we start with questions?"

I had a lot of questions, but I wasn't entirely sure how to ask them. I decided to just start firing away.

"What type of abilities does Sophie have?"

"She's an empath."

"An empath?"

"She can perceive the emotions of others better than most people and oftentimes can even influence them."

"What about Diane?"

"Diane can see past events."

"Can she see it on demand?"

"No. We only see what we need to. Sometimes you can ask to see certain things. Other times unimportant visions work their way into your mind, but none of us are strong enough to completely control when we see visions or get feelings."

"What about you? Can you only see the future?"

"I can see small pieces of the future, but I rarely see things about myself or my family. I sometimes get vague feelings about things but nothing significant. I can also find things if I have something to touch. It's called psychometry."

I paused, digesting this. "And what about me?"

She shifted. "Well, from what you've said, it sounds like you're a medium, someone who can see spirits."

A medium? But I'd only seen two ghosts before. "I must not be a very good one," I said, wondering if that was true. A small part of me knew that it probably wasn't.

My mother raised her eyebrows. "Crystal, you have a natural ability, but using your abilities takes a lot of practice. Everyone is born with the ability to be psychic, but even if you're like us, born with a more natural connection to the other side, it takes practice to learn how to control and use your abilities."

"So let's practice."

"What?"

"Let's practice. I want to get better. I don't want this to scare me, because when I saw Olivia, I almost pissed my pants, Mom. I want to help Olivia."

The words shocked even me. Is that why I was so eager to learn about this? My heart felt for Olivia; it really did. I knew by the look in her eyes that she needed help and that only I could help her.

"You didn't see her in here the other night, did you?" I asked my mother.

"No," she admitted. "With all of us put together, I was sure we could at least talk with her. But we just didn't have it in us."

With this, realization struck me like a ton of bricks. "Why were you even trying to contact her?"

My mother dropped her head with shame and avoided my gaze. "I feel really bad about it."

"What, Mom? Why does she need help?"

"It's just, I wasn't supposed to hear. I was eavesdropping."

"On who? What did you hear?" My voice was full of urgency even though the situation wasn't that dramatic. But I just had to *know*.

"I overheard Tammy talking to Sheryl about Olivia at one of our festival meetings. When I heard Olivia's name, I stopped and eavesdropped on them even though it was supposed to be a private conversation."

"What did she say?"

"She said that she was scared for her daughter. She admitted that she was having a hard time moving on. She said she could feel her daughter, like she was still here and hadn't made it to heaven yet." My mom pressed her lips together. "I know I have no place in this, but I just knew when she said this that Olivia needed help moving on…"

"And you thought you could help her," I finished. "Mom, don't feel bad. I think it *is* your place because of what you can do. You have a responsibility to help people in these kinds of situations."

"I don't know, though," my mom said. "I can't even see ghosts."

"Well, if you don't have a responsibility to Olivia, then I do. She asked me for help, and I *can* see ghosts."

CHAPTER 10

"This isn't working," I complained.

Mom and I had cleared a space in the break room and were sitting cross legged on the floor. It had been nearly 20 minutes of dead silence and darkness, all while focusing on my fingers to clear my mind. I didn't feel anything. My mom was trying to get me to open my mind so that I could better use my abilities, but I didn't feel any shift in energy or divine enlightenment.

"How's this supposed to help me become a better psychic?"

My mother didn't move from her meditative position and spoke in a calm voice. "The best way to contact the other side is to clear your mind."

This was a horrible first lesson. I had done all I could to relax my body, but I didn't feel any more psychic than when I entered the room.

"It takes time," she informed me.

Meditation gave my mind too much time to wander.

"Mom, how can all of you—Sophie, Diane, and you—be psychic? Isn't it super rare?"

She finally shifted and pulled herself up from the floor, flipping the light on. She took a seat next to me. "Yes, it is very rare, but we found each other."

"How?" I asked.

"At college. Somehow we just ended up together and eventually shared our secrets." She smiled at the memories. "It was like fate. We even called our little group 'The Sensitive Society' because we all had abilities. Together we learned how to use them."

"So that's why you moved here and started this shop? Because you were all psychic?"

"Pretty much."

"But why Peyton Springs?"

"Well, Sophie grew up here. We thought it'd be a great place to raise kids. Plus, it's a good place for business."

"Why?"

"Sophie's family moved here a long time ago, so there's a lot of psychic blood in the area. Lots of people come in for our more 'special products.'"

"Special products?" I asked warily.

"Yeah, like the real deal. Things that real psychics would use."

Suddenly their extra back room full of herbs made sense.

"Mom, if you're psychic and I'm psychic, was Grandma psychic?"

She scoffed. "No, your grandma wasn't psychic. *My* grandma was psychic, but it skipped a generation with my mom."

"And you thought it skipped a generation with me? Does it always do that?"

"Not always," she answered. "Sometimes it skips a generation. With some generations, abilities can manifest more powerfully than normal." She pressed her lips together in thought.

I didn't care to ask more questions because I already had enough to think about. I had sat in this room on the hard floor long enough. I shifted and stood. "Can we have a break, Mom? Maybe we can do this some other time this week."

We returned home, my crystal ball in my hands, and decided to have macaroni and cheese for lunch. "I'll stand here and make sure you don't burn the water, and you can make sure I don't add any salt to the noodles," I teased as we prepared our lunch.

We both moved around the kitchen in sync. For some reason, I felt a deeper connection to my mother. Perhaps it was the bond that we now shared with our abilities, even if I wasn't sure what I was capable of yet. Our macaroni wasn't terrible.

Mom and I spent some time surfing the Internet for wedding ideas, and then I took the rest of the day to finish cleaning my room. When I felt confident in my new pristine space, I crossed my legs and tried meditating again, plopping myself down at the foot of my bed. I attempted to open my mind, but I didn't know what I was searching for. *Should I try contacting Olivia? Is that a good idea to do on my own? Maybe I could look into my future. Yep. Fortune and fame for sure.* I laughed at myself. *I don't even want fame. A good fortune would be nice, though.*

Once my mind started to wander too far, I gave up on my attempts to meditate. When I looked up, I noticed the crystal ball sitting on my desk. I pulled it down and placed it next to me on the floor and pretended to look into it, but since I didn't know what to look for, I didn't see anything, and it didn't glow. *How will I ever learn to use my abilities?*

I gave up, exhausted, and crawled under the covers. I twirled my owl pendant around in my fingers until I fell asleep.

～

On Monday morning I met up with Emma straight on time. I expected her to ask about the engagement, but she didn't say anything.

"Emma, are you okay?"

She didn't answer but rather kept her head low as she watched her feet pound against the pavement.

"Emma," I prodded, concern thick in my voice.

"What?" She looked up at me, dazed. "Yeah."

"You okay?"

"Yeah, I'm fine. Why?"

"Don't you want to know about Mom and Teddy?"

"Oh, is there something more to tell?"

"No, I guess not," I admitted, "but Teddy gave me this." I held out my owl pendant to her.

She glanced at it and then looked back at her feet. "Pretty."

What was going on with Emma? Something was clearly bothering her.

I went through my day in a typical state of complete boredom. Having to do worksheets and read textbooks on my own did not interest me, so I took this opportunity to work on my abilities. I started out small, calming my body through meditation while focusing on different people in the classroom. Now that I knew what I was looking for, knowledge came easy to me.

By the end of the day, I knew that Mr. Hall would win $500 at the casino this weekend but spend $1,000. I knew where Mrs. Graham had lost her good pair of reading glasses, which were behind the Lucky Charms in the cupboard. And I knew that Lori the Librarian lied to students about her age. She was actually 52, not 45.

I thought a lot about Olivia, too. Would she try to contact me again? Would I be able to help her? What could she possibly want?

When I found my seat next to Emma and Derek at lunch, Emma was the one sifting through her potatoes today.

"You okay?" Derek asked Emma.

I shook my head at him in warning when she didn't hear him. I knew I shouldn't have done it, but when Derek left to dump his tray, I opened my mind and relaxed my body, focusing on Emma. The noise in the cafeteria made it difficult to figure out what was bothering her. Even so, I knew exactly what had happened before Derek returned to his seat.

I stared wide-eyed at Emma, unable to believe what I'd just seen. She didn't notice me staring. When Derek started talking, I returned to the present and continued our conversation.

"Uh," Derek started nervously, changing the subject. "What are you dressing up as for the Halloween festival?"

I almost didn't want to deal with this because I was too focused on Emma, but I didn't want to get too far into her business. I needed to give her time until she was ready to tell me herself. I tore my mind off her and looked into Derek's bright blue eyes as an anchor.

I shrugged. "I don't have any ideas yet. My mom has a box

of costumes, so I guess I'll find something in there. What are you going as?"

"Well, I was kind of thinking..." he glanced down at his tray, avoiding my gaze. "Maybe if you didn't have a costume idea, we could do a type of duo thing or something." He paused. "I don't know, I thought it'd be creative."

"What about Emma?" I asked, glancing at her, yet she was still in a daze.

"Uh, yeah, sure. We could do some sort of trio thing."

"We could go to my mom's shop before the game tomorrow and pick something out," I suggested.

Derek dropped his shoulders. "I have to babysit my twin sisters before the game tomorrow because my mom has an appointment and my dad will be working. How about we check out the costumes before the game on Thursday?"

"Sounds great."

"Emma," Derek tried, attempting to get her attention.

"Huh, what?" she replied, looking up.

"Want to go pick out costumes for the festival on Thursday night?"

"Uh, yeah, sure. Sounds like fun."

Emma was not at the top of her game at volleyball practice. I knew exactly why, but I didn't want to say anything. Emma needed her space, and how would she react if I told her I was psychic? I thought she'd believe me, but I didn't think she needed that right now. Maybe I'd tell her tomorrow when the weight of the world wasn't hanging on her shoulders.

"Call the ball, girls," Coach Amy yelled when Emma made another mistake. It was certainly not her day.

When I arrived home, I immediately went to my mother.

"Do you think I should say something?"

"Crystal, I think if Emma wanted you to know, she would have told you."

"But she's so down about it, Mom. I want to help."

"Just give her some time." I knew my mom was right. "You shouldn't have been snooping around anyway."

"I just wanted to know what was bothering her!" I defended.

"If you do stuff like that, she's going to have a hard time trusting you."

"Do you know that for a fact?" I challenged.

"I know that if Emma wanted you to know, she would have told you. That's all I'm saying."

I crawled into bed cursing my mother for being right. I curled up into a small ball, feeling guilty for using my talents to figure out why Emma was upset. My mom was right. That was private. I had abused my abilities.

CHAPTER 11

When I met up with Emma on Tuesday, she seemed to be feeling better. I knew she wasn't over the issue—she wouldn't be for a long time—but I knew she was going to have a better day than she had yesterday.

"Won't it be weird that Teddy will be your dad?" Emma asked on our walk to school.

"I guess I hadn't really thought of it like that. I mean, he'll still be Teddy. I won't call him Dad."

She wrinkled her nose. "It's still going to be weird with him living there and everything."

"I don't know. I think it will be cool having Teddy live with us. I like him. Plus, he makes really good food."

Emma nodded her head in agreement.

We met up with Derek before the final bell rang and all walked to class together. Emma was still on the topic of my mother's marriage when we entered the classroom and took our seats.

"Yeah, that's got to be a big change," Derek agreed.

I shrugged. "I don't know. Teddy spends a lot of time with us anyway. He just doesn't sleep at our house."

"When are they getting married?" Derek asked. "And am I invited?"

I rolled my eyes at him. "They haven't set a date, and I'm sure you'll be invited, Derek. If you're not, you can be my date, but I'll be sure you're on the guest list."

He smiled at that.

"And me," Emma chimed in. "Make sure I'm on the guest list, too. Then we can *triple date.*" She shot Derek a glance that I couldn't quite read.

"Yes, you'll both be invited. I'm sure your parents will be, too." When I said this, I immediately regretted it, but when I looked at Emma, she didn't seem fazed by it. She just smiled and opened her textbook.

When I got to our table at lunch, Derek and Emma were arguing again.

"Wait, Dustin is dating Haley... or Rachel?" Derek asked.

"Actually," I intervened, ready to set the record straight, "Dustin broke up with Haley to date Rachel, and Rachel broke up with Brandon to date Dustin, but now Rachel is cheating on Dustin with Brandon, and Haley hates Rachel for taking her boyfriend."

They both stared at me with wide eyes. Crap. How did I even know all that? It just came out.

Emma grabbed for me, her nails digging into my arm. "We need to talk." Emma forced me to abandon my food as she dragged me to the bathroom and quickly checked the stalls to make sure they were empty.

"How did you know all that?" she hissed.

I honestly wasn't entirely sure. *Should I just tell her I heard it through the grape vine, or is this my chance to tell her about my abilities?* I thought.

"I—I just said it so you guys would stop arguing," I lied.

She shook her head. "No, you didn't. *I* know, but how did you know?"

Honestly, I didn't care who was dating who, but Emma was more into the social politics of high school.

"Wait, how did you know?" I accused.

"Becca told me at practice. Oh, the perks of being on Varsity," she mused.

"Look, Emma, it doesn't matter how I know about Dustin and Rachel." I stalled, unsure if this was the right time to admit about my abilities.

"Yes, it does," she said, digging her fingernails deeper into my arm. "Becca told me that in the strictest confidence. If people know you know, they're going to think I told you because we're best friends."

"Don't worry. I won't tell anyone that I know about it," I promised, and I really meant it, mostly because I didn't care who was dating who.

"Are you not telling me because you're mad that I didn't spill the beans to you? I didn't think you cared. But seriously, who told you?"

I sighed. "I don't care, and no, I'm not mad at you for not telling me. You can keep your gossip to yourself."

"Tell me," she begged.

I wanted to tell her I was psychic so badly, but I didn't think it was the time or the place. I took the next few moments to weigh the costs and benefits of telling her. I thought about my mother's bravery when she had told Teddy, and I tried to muster up the same level of courage.

"Fine." I caved. Even if this wasn't the time, my need to

confide in her overruled that logic. I lowered my voice even though no one was around. "I'm psychic."

She rolled her eyes. "Seriously. Just tell me."

"I am serious."

Emma narrowed her eyes at me.

"I don't know how I know. I just do. Now will you please let go of my arm?" I pulled away from her, happy to have my arm back.

She pursed her lips and crossed her arms. "Come on. I know you probably promised someone not to tell, but I'm your best friend. You can tell me anything."

"Emma," I looked her dead in the eyes. "I'm being serious. I just know things, okay?"

"Prove it," she challenged. "Either prove you're psychic or tell me how you knew about Dustin and Rachel." She stuck her hand behind her back. "How many fingers am I holding up?"

"Two," I answered automatically.

"Lucky guess."

"No. I can see your fingers in the mirror."

She glanced over at the mirror, embarrassed. I let out a giggle. Emma joined in until we were engaged in a full on laughing fit.

I finally composed myself. "Look, Emma. I couldn't care less about who's dating who at this school, but I care about you. If you don't believe I'm psychic, then how do I know that your parents are getting divorced when you refused to open up to me yesterday?"

Emma's face fell and she gawked at me. Tears threatened her eyes. Should I have said that, or did I make a mistake?

"I—I'm sorry," she said quietly, her eyes still fixed on mine. "I just found out."

I pulled Emma into a hug. She didn't struggle away from

me. "It's okay. I'm sorry I used my abilities to figure out what was bothering you. I won't do it again, okay?"

I felt Emma tremble in an attempt to hold back her sobs. A tear fell gently from her eye, and she wiped it away quickly.

"How did you know that? My parents wouldn't have said anything."

"I told you. I'm psychic."

Emma gave a half-hearted smile. "You sound crazy, you know that?"

I shrugged like it didn't bother me. "As long as you believe me."

She glared at me again in skepticism. "I'm not sure."

"Remember your copy of *Charlotte's Web* you lent to Derek a while back?"

Her eyes lit up. "Only my favorite book of all time!"

"It's in his pencil case in his locker, shoved in the back behind his books." Derek's locker was such a mess, I didn't know how he found anything in there. "Even Derek doesn't know he has it, so how would I know that if I wasn't psychic?"

"That little—I knew he didn't give it back to me. I have to get him to open his locker. If it's not there..." She didn't finish. I suspected it was because she couldn't think of a good enough threat.

"It'll be there, Emma, but I have to go to the bathroom." I turned to the stall and then back to her. "And Emma, please don't tell anyone. Not even Derek."

Emma rushed off as I entered one of the stalls.

When I was done and at the sink washing my hands, I noticed motion in the mirror. I looked up to see one of the stall doors opening. I swung around to find Justine Hanson standing in front of me, her dark hair perfect and jeans skin-tight. I hadn't heard her come in. Did she come in the same time Emma left, or had she been there all along? How much had she heard?

She stared at me and crossed her arms across her body as she leaned against the stall.

"Um… hi," I said, hoping to relieve the tension in the air. Her intense glare made me very uncomfortable.

"In case you're wondering, I heard everything you said to Emma." Her tone was difficult to read. It came off as a confusing cross between condescending and kind.

"I was just joking around," I tried, but my hands were trembling under the stream of water as I said it. I hoped this would convince her. I did not want this spreading around school and having to relocate because of being a "witch."

She moved over to the sink and twisted the faucet to wash her hands at the same time I turned to dry mine. "No, you weren't."

"Come on," I argued. "You don't really believe I'm psychic."

She shrugged. "I don't know. Maybe I don't have to believe it."

"Then why do you care?" I asked, crossing my arms over my own body to appear more confident.

She shut off the faucet and turned to me.

"Because whether you're psychic or not, Emma was genuinely surprised at what you knew. You must be a pretty good detective."

Crap. What did she want? Didn't my mother warn me this would happen if I told people?

"Not really," I tried, but she was so intimidating with her superior attitude and four-inch heels.

Justine grabbed a paper towel to dry her hands. "I need your help." She wasn't asking, she was demanding. "Meet me at my locker after school, okay?" She tossed her paper towel in the garbage and turned to leave.

"And what if I won't help you?" I challenged. It's not that I didn't want to help Justine. After all, she had always been friendly, even if she was currently frightening me on some level. The thing was that I didn't want this getting out the way it had on my mother. I didn't want a repeat of kindergarten. But what if she was in trouble and *did* need my help? Could I refuse that?

She turned back to me, her hand on the door. "If you don't at least *try* to help me, I'll tell the entire school that you're psychic. I know you don't want that, do you?"

No, I didn't.

"Oh, and one more thing," she said with a smile I couldn't quite read. "Don't tell anyone you're helping me."

There was nothing I could do but meet her at her locker after school and find out what she had in store.

CHAPTER 12

*W*hen I walked back to our lunch table, my mind was still on Justine. I always thought Justine was a nice person, but she seemed so menacing in the bathroom. My hands were trembling at the threat. Would she really tell the whole school if I didn't help her?

Honestly, I tried to rationalize with myself, *how bad could it be? Maybe she just wants me to help her find something she lost. But then again, she told me not to tell anyone. Does that mean whatever she wants me to do is really bad?* I couldn't seem to set my thoughts straight and ease my anxiety.

"Oh, my gosh!" Emma squealed when I reached the table, pulling herself from an embrace with Derek. She was bouncing up in her seat, holding out the light blue book toward me. I sat next to her. She leaned over to me and whispered so only the two of us could hear. "It was right where you said it was."

Derek rolled his eyes from the opposite side of the table. "I don't know how Emma knew where to look, but she made me open my locker so she could find the darn thing. I was sure I gave it back to her."

I picked up my fork and poked at my food, my thoughts still on Justine. What was going to happen after school?

"Crystal." Derek snapped his fingers in front of my face. "Don't you agree?"

"Uh, yeah, whatever." I didn't know what I was agreeing to, but it kept the conversation going between Derek and Emma. I was grateful when I didn't have to weigh in.

The final bell for the school day set off an alarm in my body, causing my heart to pound. Why couldn't I just look into the future and see what Justine was going to ask so I could either relieve this anxiety or avoid her altogether?

"Hey," Emma started nervously when we met after school. I was crouched down at my locker. Emma stood above me and twisted a dark curl around her finger. "Do you mind if I hang out at your house before the game?"

We had a home game tonight, which meant we had a few hours of free time.

"Sure," I shrugged, hoping it would hide my anxiety. I needed to meet with Justine. "Can I just go grab something from my gym locker?" I lied. "I'll meet you in the commons."

"Are you lying to me?" She narrowed her eyes accusingly.

"No. Why would you say that?"

"Because your eyebrow is twitching."

My hand flew up to my eyebrow. Oh, no. It really was twitching. "I'm not lying," I lied again.

"Why don't I just come with you?"

"No!" I practically shouted. "I—I mean, it's kind of personal."

"Oh," Emma said, elongating the word to show she understood. She winked. "Gotcha. So you're finally a woman?"

I let out a gasp and glanced around. "Emma!" I scolded.

She laughed. "Okay. I'll see you in the commons."

Students had fled the halls quickly to escape school, so they were empty when I made it to Justine's locker. I wasn't entirely sure which one was hers, but I had a general idea.

When I arrived, Justine wasn't there. I glanced around frantically, hoping to spot her. Had I taken too much time? Was she already on her way to telling the entire school my secret? It would only take a quick text to say, "Crystal Frost is a freak," to spread like a wildfire. At least Emma and Derek would stand by my side.

Just as I was about to turn and flee in hopes of finding her before she could tell anyone, I saw her coming down the hall. She had a notebook in her hand, and her heels clicked against the floor as she rushed up to me.

"I'm so sorry. I had to talk to Mrs. Flick about an assignment." Her voice emulated a tone of friendship. It was like she was a completely different person from the girl I spoke with in the bathroom earlier. She was beaming with excitement and energy.

Justine twisted her locker combination as she spoke. "I'm so glad you're helping me with this. I've been thinking about you all day and how we're finally going to resolve this issue." She sounded like I had agreed to help her decorate for prom or something. She was far more excited than I'd expected.

She continued jabbering at a million miles per hour as she dug around in her locker. "You see, I've been trying to investigate this for like a year, but I just can't find any proof, and Kelli won't tell me anything."

"Hold up," I said, stopping her. "I may be..." I glanced

around, and even though I didn't see anyone, I lowered my voice. "Psychic. But that doesn't mean I have any idea what you're talking about."

Justine spoke softly and cocked a finger for me to come in close. Then she told me everything she knew.

~

I didn't believe it. I just couldn't. Justine thought Nate was abusing Kelli, but they looked so happy together. They had the kind of relationship every girl in the school longed for. Was it possible that the school's hottest couple wasn't so hot at all?

"I've seen the bruises," Justine had told me matter-of-factly. "But Kelli always makes excuses and says she tripped or it was from sports or whatever. That's why she always changes in the stalls before practice. She doesn't want anyone to see. It's not just that, though. Everything about her is different. She's more reserved than ever before."

"Why are you even telling me this?" I asked.

"Because I need you to help me get proof. If we don't do something, he's probably going to kill her. I've done everything I can. I talked to Kelli, but she denies it. I told her parents, but they think Nate's an angel. I even tried to turn him in, but since Kelli denied it, the police said there wasn't anything they could do. I've never seen him hit her, but I've seen how nasty he can be. Once I was riding in the car with them and Nate called her a 'fucking bitch' just because we took a wrong turn and she was supposed to be navigating. It wasn't even a big deal. He's really smart about it, too, putting on a façade in front of everyone and hitting her only where her clothes can hide it."

She glanced around and lowered her voice even further

until she was whispering. "Last summer, he must have done something really bad to her arms because she wore long sleeves for like two weeks and wouldn't come out boating with me. I haven't seen her put on a swimming suit since she met him. Sometimes she doesn't even wear her spandex shorts at games but puts on long athletic shorts instead."

Strangely enough, I had noticed that, but wearing spandex shorts wasn't a requirement for our uniform as long as the shorts were black. Could it be that she was hiding something under her shorts?

"It's only getting worse," she told me. "I love her like a sister, but we've hardly spoken since the fundraiser. In fact, we've hardly spoken all school year outside of volleyball practice. It's like something happened between them last summer. There were a few weeks there when I didn't even *see* her, let alone talk to her. Nate has more control over her than ever. She does whatever he says, and he doesn't want her hanging out with me. If you knew her like I do, you'd see that she's scared of him."

Justine sighed. "I think he used to be a nice guy, but after his parents divorced, he just became dark. And now, it's like he's got this god complex and thinks he can do whatever he wants without consequences. Like he thrives on power over women or something." She paused. "It's disgusting."

I couldn't figure out why Justine was confiding in me. Did she really think I could help her? I hardly knew how to use my abilities, and I was still trying to figure them out so that the next time Olivia showed up I could figure out what *she* needed from me, too. And then there was Emma, who I was really hoping to speak with about her parents' divorce. With school, volleyball, and everything else piled on top of that, it seemed like so much responsibility falling on me at once. Suddenly, the idea of being psychic made me want to run away from who I really was, but hadn't I said I was supposed to help people?

With this, I caved. "What do you want me to do?" I was concerned. I really was. At the same time, I honestly wasn't sure if I could help. I'd found out a few minor things about people by concentrating on them, but was I able to really know something this serious? Besides, where would I get the "proof" Justine needed? We couldn't go to the police with a psychic vision as our only proof.

"I want you to look into it, okay? Try to figure something out so we can save Kelli."

"Look, Justine. I don't even really know how to use my abilities. I'm sorry, but I don't know if I can help you."

She stared at me with a pout that even I couldn't refuse. I wasn't sure if it was an act or not, but I had to remind myself that if I didn't at least try, she was going to tell the whole school and I might be bullied out of town. I couldn't risk that with my mom's business.

"Fine," I gave in. "I'll try, but I can't make any promises."

She smiled, and then in a shocking moment, she pulled me into an embrace. "Thank you so much, Crystal."

CHAPTER 13

"Wʜat took you so long?" Emma complained when I finally reached the commons.

I didn't want my eyebrow to start twitching again. Emma was too good at telling when I was lying. We'd known each other far too long.

"I was talking to Justine," I answered truthfully.

"Justine Hanson? About what?" Emma seemed suspicious and rightfully so. I could probably count on one hand the amount of times I'd talked to Justine in the past.

I bit my lip nervously but quickly stopped so that she wouldn't notice. "She wanted help… with homework."

"Why would she ask you? You're not even in any of her classes."

I shrugged. "She just needed a second opinion." That wasn't a complete lie.

I was still nervous and overwhelmed with all the responsibility my new powers put on me, but I wasn't going to let that ruin a great time with Emma, so I put on a smile. "Come on," I said. "We need some girl talk."

On the way back to my house, I got Emma to open up about her parents' divorce. She told me about how she was sad to see her family break up but that it wasn't as bad as it sounded. She said her parents had tried marriage counseling, but they just couldn't stand each other anymore and had separated.

"But I don't want to talk about my parents. I want to know more about you and this whole psychic thing."

I smiled out of nervousness. What could I say to her about it? "Emma, I don't even know that much about it myself. I'm just learning."

"So, can you tell my future? Like if anyone is going to ask me to prom this year?"

I rolled my eyes at her. "Yeah, it doesn't work that way."

She kicked at a rock. "Aw, shucks."

When we reached my house, Emma went straight to the kitchen. "What should we have before the game?" she called, and I could already hear her opening and closing cabinets. I heard the buzz of the freezer as she opened it, and I knew she had found the frozen pizza.

We put the pizza in the oven and went to my room.

"Oh, no," Emma stopped in my doorway, alarmed.

"What?" I cried, afraid of what had scared her.

She turned to me, an expression of terror fixed on her face as she grabbed my shoulders and shook me. "Who are you, and what have you done with Crystal?" She swung around and pointed to my room. "I can see your floor!"

I laughed. "Don't scare me like that!"

"Seriously, though," she said as she plopped down on my bed. "Your room looks nice."

"I usually keep it clean," I defended, "but I've been busy for like two months with school and volleyball."

"And I haven't? I manage to keep my room clean." She was

right, and that was part of the reason I liked staying at her place better.

"Oh. My. Gosh." Emma's eyes widened as she caught a glimpse of something across the room. "What is that?" She pointed to the crystal ball on my dresser.

"Oh, that," I said nonchalantly. "Nothing." But I knew it wasn't nothing. I took the few steps over to my dresser and picked up the ball.

"Are you, like, into dark magic?"

"Dark magic? No!" I pulled the ball close to me in a protective embrace. "I just saw it at Divination and thought it looked neat." I returned the ball back to its stand and stepped back to admire it.

"But can you, like, look into it and see the future?"

I laughed. "No. Not yet at least. I don't know how to use it."

"This is so cool."

"What is?"

"That you might be psychic. You're like a superhero."

"It's not a question of 'might,' Emma. I *am* psychic." I almost wanted to argue the fact along with her and refuse my abilities and the responsibility of it, but I just couldn't do that.

"Come on," Emma said, sitting up in my bed. "We'll play a game."

Really? Was she serious? I knew Emma wouldn't give up until I played. "Okay, but I won't promise that it will work."

Emma shifted excitedly. "I'm going to take an object and hide it somewhere, and you're going to find it."

"Emma, I don't even know how to do that."

She held out a finger to me and made noises until I stopped speaking. "It's just a game, okay? You stay here." She leapt from my bed and left the room, closing my door behind her.

Ugh. I plopped down on my bed and placed my arm over my eyes. She was going to find the smallest thing to hide and put it in an impossible place to find. I wasn't going to win this game.

I wanted to cry. So much was happening lately with Olivia, Justine, and everything else related to my abilities. But I held myself together.

Emma came back a few minutes later and announced that I could start looking. I didn't move from my spot.

"Well, aren't you going to look for it?"

"I am," I teased. I'd never found things before except her copy of *Charlotte's Web* in Derek's locker. Then I remembered how I had found her CD. Maybe I *did* have a gift for finding.

"Even with psychic powers, you'll never find it," she said smugly.

Suddenly, I was up to the challenge.

My mom had told me she could find things. *I can also find things if I have something to touch. It's called psychometry.*

I sat up in my bed and held my hand out.

"What?" Emma asked.

"Come here. I need to see your hand."

"My hand?"

"Yeah, the one that held whatever you hid."

I gripped her hand and closed my eyes, concentrating hard on the object. Within seconds, I knew exactly what and where it was. I hopped up from the bed.

"Not-uh. You do not know where it is." Emma raced after me.

I headed down the hallway and pounded down the stairs to the laundry room. There were two laundry baskets full of clothes, one with towels and one with whites. I picked up the one full of whites and dumped its contents onto the floor. Emma stood next to me as I did this, her eyes wide and her mouth open.

I only had to toss aside two pieces of clothing before I found Emma's sock with its signature pink stripe in the mess. I reached for her ankle and pulled up on her pant leg. She was missing one of her socks. I held it up triumphantly, and a victorious grin spread across my face that made me—if only for a moment—slightly prouder of my abilities.

She frowned and snatched the sock out of my hand before storming back up the stairs. Was she mad at me?

"Emma," I called after her, but she didn't say anything back. *What did I do wrong?*

I slowly walked out of the laundry room and found Emma at the top of the stairs putting her sock back on her foot.

"Emma," I said softly. "Are you mad at me?"

"Yes," she answered crossly. When she was done tying her shoe, she planted her foot on the stair and crossed her arms, giving me the evil eye. "I'm mad because hide and seek is never going to be any fun again." She couldn't help it when her lips curled into a smile.

When I realized she wasn't actually angry with me, I approached her and gave her a hug. "You always liked to be the finder anyway. I can hide from now on."

We laughed together.

"I'm not mad at you, Crystal. I think it's awesome that you're a superhero."

"I'm not a superhero. I'm just psychic. It's even weird to say that. I'm still getting used to it."

"Well, it's pretty cool." Emma stopped and sniffed the air. "Do you smell something burning?"

We exchanged an alarmed glance and bolted for the

kitchen together. Smoke was coming from the oven. Our pizza was burnt to a crisp because we'd forgotten to set the timer.

"Maybe we should just stick with microwaveable food," I suggested.

We ate hot pockets before heading to our volleyball game. Justine kept throwing me nervous glances as if to ask if I'd found anything out yet. I sent her back a look that said, *Sorry, nothing yet.*

Both the JV and the Varsity won.

CHAPTER 14

That night, Olivia came to me in my dreams. I only saw her face for a moment, but she whispered something to me. "Help her," she said, but I woke up not knowing who "her" was. I felt a wave of guilt rush over me. I knew I should have been focusing more attention on Olivia than on other things. She needed me.

When I woke up that Wednesday, I made a list of all the people Olivia could possibly mean by "her," but I only came up with one name: Tammy Owen. Did Tammy need help moving on? I had heard she was holding together pretty well, but some people are better at hiding it than others.

I told my mother about my dream and my concerns about Tammy.

"I don't really know how to help her, sweetie. I mean, Tammy and I get along, but I'm not exactly her best friend."

"Oh." I slumped my shoulders in disappointment. I didn't know how *I* was supposed to help Tammy.

"I'll look into it," my mother promised, which made me feel a little better. "But you know what? The girls and I can get together Friday night again. Maybe we can talk with Olivia this time and see what she really needs. With you there, I'm sure it will be easier."

My mom was inviting me to a séance? *That should be interesting*, I thought.

"But don't you have to get ready for the Halloween festival for Saturday?" I asked.

"It'll be fine. We don't have to do anything for it Friday night."

"Okay, I look forward to it." Did I really mean that? The whole idea of a séance scared me yet seemed exhilarating at the same time.

That day at school, I spent most of my time focusing my energy on Kelli. I ignored my teachers as I concentrated on my breathing and tried to relax my body and connect with her, but I came up blank every time. Either there wasn't anything to find or I wasn't as powerful as I thought. Either way, I couldn't seem to get through to her.

At lunch, I spotted Kelli and Nate across the lunch room, which sparked an idea. Maybe if I focused on *him* I could find something. Since Emma and Derek kept asking my opinion about music and distracting me, I didn't have the chance to concentrate on him. To top it off, all my teachers decided to actually do something in class the rest of the day, so I didn't have the opportunity to find anything on Nate.

When it came time for volleyball practice, our last practice of the season before our final game, Justine pulled me aside in the locker room. Unfortunately, I had nothing to tell her.

"I'm trying. I really am. But I can't see anything. Maybe if I could actually talk with Kelli, but I can't just bring it up."

"Well try harder," Justine hissed. "I'm getting really worried, and you're my only hope to save my best friend."

"I'm sorry."

Just then, Kelli pushed through the door into the locker room. We both stood upright in surprise, immediately ceasing our conversation. Kelli eyed us suspiciously, but I didn't think she knew we were talking about her. How could she?

After practice, I came up with the perfect opportunity to speak to Kelli. I watched as she left the locker room. I reached into my locker and grabbed the first thing my hands found.

"I'll be right back," I told Emma.

When I caught up to Kelli, I grabbed her wrist. She swung around at the same time she took a step back to distance herself from me. I was expecting to see something, an indication of her relationship, but there was nothing. My plan failed miserably. Interestingly, though, my touch allowed me to feel her emotions. She was confused why I was there and upset about something.

"What?" she demanded when I didn't say anything.

For a moment, I couldn't remember what my plan was, and then I looked down to find a bottle of lotion in my hands. "I thought I saw you drop this." I held the bottle out to her.

"Well, it's not mine." Not only did she sound irritated, but I could feel the annoyance as energy sizzled between us.

"I'm sorry. My mistake."

Just as I was about to turn and leave, a car pulled up next to us. Kelli's emotions shifted from exasperation to something entirely confusing, a mixture of emotions that made it hard to pinpoint. A sense of love, it seemed, washed over her when she saw the car. I also took note of the fear she conveyed by the sight of it. As her pulse quickened, so did mine. I wondered for a moment if it was a family member driving the car.

"Are you okay?" I asked without thinking. It only made her widen her eyes at me in suspicion.

"I have to go," she said as she turned on her heel and flipped her hair over her shoulder.

I glanced at the driver, and even though it was getting dark, it was still light enough to see his face. Nate Williams sat in the front seat. After Kelli closed the door, he jerked his head toward me and glared, his eyes dark below his eyebrows and the muscles in his jaw tense. It sent chills up and down my spine.

He tore his gaze from me and drove off. *Holy crap. He is a bad guy, isn't he? And Kelli is afraid of him.* I turned back toward the school, discouraged that my plan didn't work. Or had it?

I didn't realize that I was frowning when I got back to the locker room.

"Are you okay?" Emma asked.

Suddenly aware of my posture, I straightened up and put a smile on my face. "I'm fine," I lied and turned away so that she couldn't see my eyebrow twitch.

"So whose house are we staying at this weekend?"

"Uh," I stalled. "This weekend? I can't this weekend." I didn't care how much Emma begged, I would not miss out on the séance this Friday. I needed to focus on Olivia, especially since I'd been neglecting her and she needed my help.

"Why not?"

I couldn't tell her, could I? I didn't know if it was right to tell Emma that Mom, Sophie, and Diane were all psychic, too. I decided to keep this one to myself.

I ducked down behind my locker door so she wouldn't see my face. "Uh, my mom kind of has a mother-daughter thing planned on Friday." That wasn't a lie. "Don't worry. I'll still be here when we turn in our uniforms and have our pizza party on Friday."

"Oh, yeah," she said, trying to hide her disappointment. "Yeah, that will be fun."

I suspected that Emma wanted to be at home as little as possible, but I had other people to help at the moment. Besides, she said that home life wasn't that bad.

When I got home, I slumped onto my bed. I wanted to cry, to relieve the overwhelming knot in my chest, but no tears came out. When I finally gave up and lifted my head, my gaze fell upon the crystal ball on my dresser. Maybe that would have some answers, but I didn't know how to use it. I thought about waiting for my mom to get home from the shop, which was staying open later and later as Halloween approached, but the longer I waited, the more I felt I needed to take my abilities into my own hands. I decided it was time to turn to the Internet for help.

I pulled Luna down from the shelf next to my bed, holding her close for comfort, and snuggled under my blanket. I flipped open my laptop and typed "How to Use a Crystal Ball" into the Google search bar. The first few sites I visited didn't help me at all, but I continued my search anyway, clicking through links and trying to find some helpful information. I got excited when I found an article that seemed to make sense. It told me to set the mood with candles or incense, let go of expectation, and to practice discipline over the conscious mind. It also noted that I should listen to the more subtle voices of the universe, whatever that meant.

I wasn't sure how this was going to go, but I decided to take a shot at it. I mean, what could it hurt? Rising from my bed, I walked into the kitchen and shuffled through a few drawers before finding a stash of candles. I gathered the tea candles and a box of matches and headed back to my room. One by one, I lit three candles. I shut off the light and placed myself in my desk chair in front of the crystal ball.

I paused for a moment, mostly out of uncertainty. I wasn't sure I would really be able to do this, but if my crystal ball could help me help others, then it was something I was willing to try.

I held the ball in my hands and stared into it for what seemed like an eternity. I didn't see anything. *Let go of expectation*, I told myself as I tried to put both Olivia and Kelli out of my mind. For a brief moment, I almost believed that the ball had no power, but when I regained control of my mind, I allowed myself to do as the website instructed and opened my mind to all possibilities.

Discipline over the conscious mind. Control yourself. Let go of expectations.

I let my mind relax as I stared deep into the crystal ball. When it started glowing, I squealed with excitement. The light dimmed in reply to my squeal, so I tried again, doing as I had done before. This time when it glowed and the glass clouded over, I didn't let my excitement get the better of me.

I stared further into it, making the connection with my ball. When I was confident in our connection, I set it back on its stand. I allowed myself to fall deeper into my trance.

The fog within the ball began to dissipate, and motion passed across it as if I were watching a scene unfold on a television screen. But when the image became clear, I didn't see Kelli or Olivia.

No expectations, I thought in the conscious part of my

mind, but I let even that thought fall as I pushed my mind to connect with the ball and find discipline over my consciousness.

The first image I saw was of a small bedroom. The walls were pink, and there was a collection of teddy bears stacked against the wall. Frilly lace curtains outlined the windows.

As the angle zoomed out, I saw her, the girl whom the room clearly belonged to. She was curled in a lump on her bed and looked cozy beneath the sheets. I couldn't see her face, but she didn't look very big.

Movement in another corner of the room caught my attention. A tall figure moved in the shadows. He was dressed in all black, so it was hard to notice him at first. He moved closer to the girl, and when he was close enough, he pounced, clasping his hand hard over her mouth so that she wouldn't scream.

The girl's eyes flew open, and the image focused on her face.

I pushed back in my chair too quickly, flinging the crystal ball to the floor. It landed on the carpet with a thud.

My heart pounded, and my hands trembled. What did that little girl have to do with me? Why did I need to see that scene? I'd seen her brown hair and big chocolate eyes in a nightmare before, but what did that mean? I knew deep down that it meant something. It wasn't about Kelli or Olivia, my intuition told me, but I couldn't help but ask myself the question: Why have I seen her twice now?

I didn't want to look into my crystal ball again, so I didn't. Instead, I wanted to toss it across the room. I held back that urge, afraid that it would break. I already felt bad about letting it fall to the floor. Questions continued to race in my mind. How could I help a little girl I didn't even know? Was the man going to hurt her? As much as I longed to do something, I didn't know enough to help. All I knew about the girl was what she looked like and her approximate age.

That's not much to go on, I thought. Besides, I had too much to deal with already and too many people to help. Why hadn't my crystal ball shown me something about Kelli or Olivia? That was what I really wanted to see—no, needed to see.

Discouraged for not finding anything to actually help anyone I knew, and not giving me enough information to help Chocolate Eyes, I blew out the candles and crawled into bed far too early, but I fell asleep instantly.

CHAPTER 15

*A*fter a sound sleep, I woke up Thursday well-rested. I still had problems to solve and a mystery from my crystal ball, yet I was relaxed and ready to take on the day.

I could hear Teddy talking to my mom from the kitchen. I quickly realized that he had spent the night. Did this mean he was already working on moving in? I didn't have a chance to check it out before I heard the front door close, indicating that he was already on his way to work.

I started the day by taking a warm shower and drying my long dirty blonde hair. The hair dryer left my hair straight, so I kept it that way, brushing it to near perfection.

"Crystal," my mother called from the other side of the house. "I have to go to work, but Teddy and I will be at your game tonight, okay?"

My heart flipped at the thought. Just one more game and the season was over, and I'd have more free time on my hands. I was excited and disappointed at the same time, but at least I would have more time to figure out my abilities and actually put them to use helping people.

"Okay, Mom. I love you."

"Love you, too. Bye!"

"Bye!" I shouted back. I gave myself a confident smile in the mirror.

Gathering my backpack and supplies for the day, I left my room and headed for the kitchen, popping a bagel in the toaster and pulling out some cream cheese from the fridge to top it with. Yum. My favorite.

I turned on the TV for a few moments to get the scoop on the weather, but when the news switched to a story about a local abduction, I turned it off. I wasn't in a mood to focus on more unfortunate mysteries than the ones I already had on my plate.

The house was quiet, and I was ready for school early, so I wiggled my way onto the counter and closed my eyes. It was bright behind my lids. I could hear the soft hum of the appliances and smell the delicious scent of a toasting bagel. It seemed so serene.

What will I learn about my abilities today? I wondered. I let my body relax as I focused on my fingertips like my mother taught me. My mind spun in an elegant dance through clouds as I concentrated on the other side to guide me in my day's decisions. I felt at peace.

In an instant, it all changed, sending me reeling toward something dangerous. A frightening roar reverberated in my ears as a shock of terror spread through my body. My bagel popped, snapping me out of it.

What was that all about? I thought as I hopped down from the countertop. My hands were still shaking and my pulse threatening as I spread cream cheese over my bagel.

It was nothing, I assured myself, but I still couldn't shake the feeling that it was a sign of something to come, that someone was coming to get me and would take me by surprise. My sense of peace shattered.

~

I met Emma at our corner, my anxiety and paranoia just above its normal level, but I didn't let it show.

The moment Emma was close enough to me, she started speaking. "I was reading last night, you know, about your kind, and I was thinking—"

"My kind?" I eyed her speculatively.

"Yeah, about psychics and stuff," she said, waving a hand nonchalantly. "I was reading that to make your powers stronger, you have to practice them, and—"

"Why?" I interrupted again. I never expected Emma to ditch me as a friend when I told her about my abilities, but I didn't expect her to be so accepting of it, either.

She shrugged. "I don't know. I guess it's just intriguing. I mean, it'd be awesome if I were psychic, but if I can't be, then it's cool that you are."

"Actually you can be. My mom said everyone's born with psychic abilities but that I just have a stronger connection to the other side or something. Like how everyone has intuition. It just takes practice, I guess."

"Ohmigosh," Emma squealed, stopping in her tracks. "We should, like, learn together, and we could *both* be psychic."

Something about the idea intrigued me. It was cool enough that I had my mom to help me, but I would be much more comfortable with Emma by my side.

"That would be really cool," I said, smiling. "But I really don't know that much about how to do it. Maybe you could talk to my mom."

I threw my hand over my mouth. Was I allowed to tell

Emma my mom is psychic? I didn't think it would hurt anything, but I should have asked my mom first.

Emma's eyes widened. "Andrea's psychic, too? I mean, a real psychic? I know she does all that fake voodoo stuff for Halloween, but she's real?"

I dropped my hand. "Well, let's just say it's not as fake as she leads people to believe."

Emma smiled. "This is going to be so awesome. When can we start?"

I bit my lip nervously. I wasn't sure if I wanted to include Emma in the séance right away. It almost seemed too much for *me*. I didn't want to overwhelm her and scare her away.

"Maybe it's best if we wait until after this weekend once we all have more free time. Then my mom will be done with the Halloween festival."

"Deal," Emma agreed.

We got to school too soon.

Emma grinned. "I'll tell you about what I read later. Maybe I could come to your house before the game again."

"Yeah, sure. That sounds great." Even as I said this, I wasn't entirely positive. I was eager for some more alone time to practice with my crystal ball again. I was hoping to see something I could use to help Olivia or Kelli.

At the same time, I wanted so badly to share my abilities with Emma, and maybe even Derek, but I didn't know what I should tell her. A wave of guilt rushed over me. I'd never hidden anything from Emma in the decade that I'd known her, so why did it seem like I was hiding so much lately?

My mind raced with thoughts of Emma and me during my morning classes, which left me little time to remember to worry about Olivia or Kelli. I was too busy day dreaming about what it would be like to share abilities with my best friend. I knew it was selfish of me, but it was hard to think of anything else when Emma kept throwing excited glances my way.

I wanted to talk about it with Emma in first period, but we were both smarter than to talk about it in front of people. I had told her to keep this to herself, and she had. On some level, I think she understood the importance.

When lunch rolled around, I met Emma and Derek at our usual spot. When my hair wouldn't stay behind my shoulders and kept falling into my food, I had to excuse myself so I could get a hair tie from my locker and put it back.

The hallway was vacant when I got to my locker. I put in my combination and reached into my backpack for a hair tie and the travel brush I kept there. I looked into my small magnetic mirror as I pulled up my hair. When satisfied, I returned my brush to its proper position.

My heart nearly jumped out of my chest when I closed my locker and found Nate Williams staring down at me, which was weird because he'd never talked to me before.

"Um… can I help you with something?" I asked. No matter how much I tried, I couldn't keep the nerves from my voice. What was he doing at my locker?

"I saw you talking to Kelli last night," he said casually as if we had been friends forever. It was hard to not look into his handsome face, a masterpiece really, but something told me that his bright eyes and grin was just a façade.

"Yeah… I just thought she dropped some lotion." My throat tightened, and my mouth dried as my pulse quickened at the encounter. I was not comfortable being in a hallway alone with him right now, no matter how friendly he was acting. A dark haze that I'd never noticed before surrounded his body as if warning me of danger. I considered running, but I decided to play it cool. *Maybe I can talk my way out of this,* I thought. *Maybe he really is being friendly.*

"She said you asked if she was okay."

"Yeah, I did. I was just concerned—"

"Concerned about what?" His tone shifted accusingly.

I took a step back, distancing myself from him.

"She said she's seen you talking to Justine. What did Justine tell you about me?"

"Nothing." I could already feel my eyebrow twitching. At least he didn't know that happened when I lied. "I was just trying to be a good friend."

"Well, don't be," he snapped.

I took another step back, larger this time, until I could feel the cool touch of my locker on my back.

Nate only came in closer, jabbing a finger in my direction. "You know, I'm so sick of people like you and Justine and Olivia getting their nose where it doesn't belong, okay?" His voice was quiet, but it was full of enough fury to make me tremble.

"I—I'm sorry. I didn't mean anything by it."

"Whatever you think you know," he snarled, still pointing a finger at my chest, "you're wrong. Kelli and I are fine."

I didn't need my psychic abilities to tell me that I wasn't wrong. The way he advanced toward me with a threatening tone told me he was used to dominating. The way he spoke his words said he had something to hide. I glanced around the hallway, but no one was going to come to my rescue. Being all alone, I decided it was best to defend myself.

"You know what," I said sternly, taking a stance. "I didn't quite believe Justine at first, but maybe she was right about you."

Crap. What did I just say? Why didn't I just play it cool?

I didn't see it coming. Suddenly, he lunged at me, pinning me against a locker. Its combination lock dug into my back. He wrapped a hand around my neck and held me in place, bending down so that his face was just inches from mine. The strange feeling I got this morning returned, and the roar rang loud in my ears, a sound that only I, a psychic, could hear.

He leaned in close so that I could feel his hot breath on the side of my face. He came in to whisper in my ear. "You mind your own fucking business, okay? Whatever happens between me and my girl doesn't concern you, so I'd advise that you stay away. If you don't," he paused for dramatic effect, which successfully quickened my pulse, "there *will* be consequences."

And then he dropped me, letting me fall into a ball at his feet. He glared down at me for a moment before walking away, a strut that showed his confidence from every angle.

I wrapped my own fingers around my neck and coughed, terrified by his threat. What was wrong with him? I pressed my head against the locker, calming my breath and slowing my heart rate. I knew I didn't need proof anymore to believe Justine's allegations toward him. But as much as I wanted it now than ever, I still didn't have anything that could save Kelli. What if I continued searching for proof, spying on him with my abilities? Would he honestly seek revenge?

With little hesitation, I decided that I would do whatever I could to prove he was a dangerous guy. I rose from the floor, clenching my fists. My eyes narrowed down the hall at his retreating figure. *Nate Williams, you just made this battle personal, and you're not going to hurt* this *girl and get away with it!*

$\mathcal{I}$ stayed silent when I got back to the lunch table, knowing full well that I couldn't tell my friends what had just happened to me. I was lucky that Derek and Emma were so great at getting in heated conversation that they didn't ask me to join in.

I only heard pieces of their discussion, but I didn't fully process it. "A girl from the elementary school… they don't know… just shouldn't happen in a town like this."

Instead, I tuned them out and stared at Kelli and Nate, intent on finding something that would prove he was a bad person.

But what *could* I do? Justine knew what was going on, yet she couldn't successfully help Kelli. No one would believe any proof I could give them, except for maybe Teddy, but there'd be no case. What if there was proof somewhere? Maybe there was a photo of Kelli's bruises. Wherever there was proof, I'd find it.

By the end of lunch, I still had nothing. I needed to find a quiet place to relax and open up my mind if I was going to find anything. I didn't honestly know when I would have that opportunity.

"Hey," Derek said as we rose from the lunch table when the bell rang. "Are we all still on for after school?"

"After school?" I asked.

"Yeah. Aren't we going to go pick out costumes?"

I glanced at Emma. I totally forgot about that, and I was really hoping to talk to Emma about what she had read up on, especially now that I was more interested in getting dirt on Nate. I really had to learn how to channel my powers.

Emma and I exchanged a glance, both disappointed that we wouldn't have the opportunity to talk about this issue for a while. I could tell she was excited to learn more about it, too.

"Yeah, I guess we all need costumes, don't we?" Emma said. "We'll head over after school, Derek."

"Ooh, I really like this one." Emma held up a sexy kitten costume.

"Emma," I complained from behind my rack. "We're supposed to be looking for something we can wear as a trio. I don't think Derek would go for wearing a skirt."

Derek turned from the rack he was looking at and eyed the costume. "Mm... I don't know, Crystal. I think it would show off my legs well."

I laughed at him. "If you say so."

"Derek, if you want to go to the festival in that costume, I won't be the one selling it to you," Diane joked from behind the counter.

I knew my mother was somewhere in the back, but I wished she was out here to help us find a great costume. We had already asked Diane for ideas, but she said Mom knew more about the costumes they had in stock.

"Maybe we could go as the three musketeers," I suggested, which made Emma crinkle her nose at the idea.

Derek turned back to his rack of costumes and headed down the aisle.

Emma watched him go. Once he was out of ear shot, she started whispering to me. "I really think you should tell him."

"Tell him what?" I asked, looking back over toward Derek.

"Tell him that you're..." She glanced around at the other customers in the store, but none of them were paying attention to us. She lowered her voice further just in case. "Psychic."

"I don't know. What if he doesn't believe me?" I glanced back at Derek. He was completely ignoring us. *But he wouldn't believe me, would he?*

"Well, I believed you."

"Yeah," I argued, "but isn't Derek's family Christian? Don't they, like, shun psychics or something?"

Emma giggled. "I don't think Derek would shun you. Especially because he likes you."

"What?" I squeaked, stealing another glance at him before lowering my voice again. "He does not."

"He *so* does."

"Oh, please," I said. "Like I haven't seen you batting *your* eyes at him. You can't get enough of arguing with that boy. Besides, I couldn't do that to either of you. I couldn't risk our friendship." I didn't have to add that I meant mine and hers as well.

She turned to another costume, shaking off my statement. "I still think you should tell him." I couldn't help but notice that she didn't argue with my accusations.

I took a deep breath. I really did want to tell Derek, but I was too nervous that he wouldn't believe me.

"I'll back you up," Emma encouraged. "I just think it would be cool if he knew, too. We wouldn't have to have secret conversations like this."

I caved, unable to refuse her logic. "Okay, we'll tell him."

"Hey, Derek," she called.

"What?" I hissed at her. "Right now?"

She shrugged. "Not necessarily. I'm just going to warm him up to the idea."

Oh, no. What did she have in mind?

"Yeah?" he asked when he made his way over to us.

Emma put on an innocent face. "You know all that stuff they have in the other room?"

They both glanced at the opposite end of the store.

"Yeah. They have crystal balls and tarot cards and stuff in there. What about it?"

Emma squinted an eye like she was thinking. "Do you believe in that kind of stuff? I mean, like for real. Do you think people can know things?"

"What? You mean, like, psychics?"

Emma nodded. "Yeah, like psychics, fortune tellers, astrologers, and whatnot."

Derek shrugged then began flipping through the costumes where I left off. "I don't know. I guess I'd have to meet one to believe it."

I was getting nervous.

Emma glanced at me, and with reluctance, I gave her a look of approval back, allowing her to divulge my secret to Derek. "But you have met one."

"Huh? I think I would remember that."

Emma looked around at the other customers again and

decided we were safe from ear shot. "Crystal's a psychic, and I'm going to be one, too," she said proudly.

Derek rolled his eyes. "Yeah, and I'm Clark Kent."

That stung at my heart a little.

"I'm serious," Emma insisted, and we both stared at him.

His eyes shifted back and forth between us, gauging our expressions. "You're serious."

I nodded.

Derek crossed his arms over his body and narrowed his eyes the same way Emma had when I told her. "Prove it."

I smirked. "Challenge accepted."

Emma and I walked to the back of the store and entered the break room so Derek could hide an object in private. He insisted that Emma come with me so that we couldn't cheat.

"Make sure to hide it really hard," Emma told him. "Crystal is really good at this game."

Emma and I sat across each other on the table in the break room.

"I did not expect him to believe us," I said.

"I don't think he does," Emma admitted. "Not quite yet. But when you find whatever he hid, he'll have to. Derek was always good at hide and seek, but you were better. You know, now I understand how you always found us so fast."

Looking back on it, I always was great at finding them.

Emma and I both jumped when the door to the break room swung open. My mother jumped back, too, and placed her hand across her heart.

"I'm sorry, girls," she said as she entered the room. "I didn't realize anyone was in here. I just need to grab a snack from my purse."

"Hey, Andrea," Emma greeted, but I knew there was more she wanted to say. "Crystal and I were thinking that sometime next week you could teach us more about being psychic."

My mother didn't miss a beat in her step. She wasn't surprised that I'd told Emma.

"I want to learn, too," Emma continued. "I did a bunch of research on different exercises you can do to enhance your abilities. That's what I wanted to talk to you about this morning, Crystal. I wanted to tell you about all these different types of exercises I found and maybe do some together." She turned her gaze toward my mother. "Crystal said that anyone can be psychic with practice. Is that true?"

"If you really want to, then yes," my mom answered. "I mean, your abilities won't be as strong as Crystal's, but we can try."

Emma fist pumped the air. Why was Emma more excited about this than I was? Was it because I'd already had a small taste of what it was like and I wasn't too excited about all the responsibility? To Emma, it was just a game, but I knew it meant more than that.

"Why don't you join us tomorrow night, Emma?" my mom offered.

"Mom!" I hadn't told Emma anything about Olivia, and my mom had to go break it to her that I'd lied.

Emma glanced from me to my mom then back at me. "What's happening tomorrow night? I thought you were having a girl's night."

My mom bit off a piece of her granola bar. "Yeah, just not the typical girl's night."

Emma looked at me for explanation.

"You didn't tell her?" my mother asked in surprise.

"Mom!" I scolded again. I didn't want her scaring off Emma, but now I was kind of stuck. I turned to Emma. "We're holding a séance."

Emma's eyes widened. "Oh, my gosh. That would be so cool! Why didn't you tell me, Crystal?" She swatted a hand at me like I was a puppy that had been bad. She looked at me expectantly.

A wave of guilt flooded over me. "I—I thought it would scare you away."

"No, it sounds totally awesome. I might even see a ghost! A real ghost!"

She looked back toward my mom. "You don't have to be psychic to join the séance?"

"Nope. The more believers, the merrier."

"So who are you holding the séance for, and why?"

Before we had a chance to explain, Derek opened the door. "I hid it," he announced.

If people kept playing this game with me, it wasn't going to be fun for me for very long. Just one quick touch of Derek's hand and I knew exactly where he'd hid it.

"You hid your pencil," I announced to add to the show before I reached into his sweatshirt hood and pulled it out. "Sneaky little..." I muttered.

Derek's eyes widened. "I thought that hiding place was genius. Now this explains why you were always so good at hide and seek."

Emma and I exchanged a glance and giggled.

"I'm still not convinced, but I will say that I'm amazed. Were you guys spying on me?" Derek glanced at his watch. "We'll have to try this again somewhere where you *can't* spy on me."

Figures, I thought. *I knew he wouldn't believe me.*

"Andrea," Derek said, "we don't have much time until we

have to get ready for the game. Do you have any suggestions on a trio costume we could wear to the festival?"

She thought about this for a moment, and then without saying anything, she led us to a rack of costumes we hadn't made it to yet.

She handed us each a hanger. Derek held up a Cat in the Hat costume, Emma a Thing 1 costume, and me a Thing 2 costume. They were perfect.

"I'll see you at your game," my mom said after we purchased our costumes.

"Okay. Love you, Mom," I said, kissing her on the cheek.

"I love you, too, Crystal." She glanced at my friends then back at me. "Can I talk to you for a minute?"

My mom led me back to the break room.

"What is it?" I asked.

She sighed. "Look, Crystal. I really respect your decision about telling Emma. I trust Emma, too, which is why I don't have a problem with it. I can sense something in her." She paused for a moment as if thinking. "But Derek?" Her eyes looked at me for an explanation.

"Mom, he's just as much my friend as Emma is."

She stared at me seriously. "Men can be..." She paused to find the right word. "Different. I just don't want to see you hurt. That's all. I'm not saying that I think Derek is a bad guy. It's just—"

I pulled her into an embrace and cut her off. "It's okay, Mom."

She hugged me back. "Okay. As long as you know what you're doing."

I smiled. "I hope so."

CHAPTER 17

e dropped off our costumes back at my house before heading out the door for our last game of the season.

After we made it to the school and Emma and I were finally alone before we had to warm up, we went back to the conversation I knew we were both dying to have.

"So who is the séance for?" Emma asked.

I took a deep breath, relieved that I could share this with her without her freaking out. "Olivia."

"What's up with Olivia?"

"I honestly don't really know. Mom said that Tammy said something about Olivia needing help, so we decided to do this to help her cross over, you know?" I wanted to tell her about Kelli and Nate, too, but Justine told me not to.

"Wow," Emma said in admiration. "You guys are so cool."

"And she kind of asked for my help," I admitted.

"Who? Your mom?"

"Well, yeah. And Olivia." I bit my lip, wondering how Emma would take this.

"You *saw* her?"

I shrugged like it was nothing. "Yeah, I saw her three times and once in a dream. She wants me to help someone, but I don't know who. I think it's her mom. Like she wants her mom to get over her death or something."

"Well, I guess we'll find out tomorrow night. Oh, and my best friend is so *cool*."

I smiled at this. "No, Emma, you're cool." I really meant this. Who could have any better friends?

Emma and I returned to the gym for warm ups. I caught a glimpse of my mom and Teddy in the stands and waved at them, glad that they were able to make my game. I didn't just have cool friends; I had an awesome family, too.

The game was intense. The score stayed close the entire way. We won the first set and lost the second. Coach put me in for the last set, and I was all over the court at the top of my game. The last point of the game, when we led the score, played through my senses in slow motion. Betsy served the ball, then a girl on the other team hit it back over on the first hit. Emma dove for the ball in the back, allowing Jenna to set it up perfectly so that I could jump and, with all my arm strength, spike the ball to the other side. The ball hit the gym floor, and the home team burst into applause. We won our last game of the season, and it felt fantastic.

As our team exited the court to allow the Varsity to warm up, Justine caught ahold of me and pulled me aside.

"Anything?" she asked.

Even with Nate threatening me earlier, the fun I'd had with Derek and Emma after school took my mind off of it. Boy, did I feel like a bad person at that moment. I should have been paying more attention to this issue rather than picking out Halloween costumes.

I shook my head. "Nothing of proof yet, but something did happen." Then I told her about how Nate threatened me.

"That guy really has issues. I'm really sorry that happened to you, Crystal, but we have to do something soon. Kelli's getting more distant, and I'm afraid it's getting worse. I can't even text her without him telling her what to say back to me. He's so controlling."

"I'll do my best," I promised, and I really meant it.

I found a seat next to my mom and Teddy on the bleachers. We all stayed and watched the Varsity play and were excited when the coach played Emma and she killed two serves in a row, but I was paying more attention to Kelli as she moved around the court. I caught a glimpse of Nate in the stands, but I was too afraid to watch him, scared that he'd notice I was staring.

Oh, Kelli, I thought, *how am I supposed to help you if you won't even let your best friend help?*

The game continued, and the Hornets stayed in the lead. The whole crowd drew a breath in sync when a girl from the other team spiked the ball. It soared through the air quick as lighting and smacked Kelli in the face, knocking her to the ground. She sat in the middle of the court and covered her face with her right hand while her left supported her weight.

Suddenly, I wasn't sitting on the bleachers in a crowded gym anymore. The scene shifted around me. The gym dissolved, and a bedroom with white walls and sports posters replaced it. I spun around, confused. Where was I?

When my eyes adjusted, I saw two figures sitting on the bed in the middle of the room. Both were facing away from me but seemed strangely familiar. The guy had blonde hair that was long enough to show a gentle wave to it. He seemed tall and athletic. The girl appeared young with long, dark blonde hair. She had her arm around him like she was comforting him. His head fell as if he was crying.

"I just don't know what's going to happen," the guy said. I knew that voice. He seemed younger than just moments before, but I knew it was Nate Williams.

I walked around the bed to the other corner of the room so I could see their faces. For a moment, I was afraid the couple would react to my presence, but I reminded myself that this wasn't really happening.

Sure enough, I was watching Nate and Kelli talk, only they were younger, and Kelli's hair was a darker shade of blonde. I was looking into the past. It must have been when they first started dating. Each of them had a younger look in their eyes.

Nate's jaw was tight, and he had a scowl plastered on his face. What was he so angry about?

"People get divorced all the time, Nate," Kelli said to comfort him. "I mean, my parents are divorced. Olivia's parents are divorced. It's really not that bad."

"Not that bad?" he practically yelled, his nostrils flaring. "My dad cheated on my mom, and now his whore mistress has split up my family. We had it so great until *she* came along. Now nothing will ever be the same." He rose from the bed in rage, pacing back and forth as he ranted. "My mom's too depressed to even take care of me and my brothers anymore. I mean, how can I trust her after what she did last week? You think that's not bad? Downing pills because this family is so fucked up. That's not *that* bad?" He came so close to her face that I was sure she might burst into flames from his rage.

Despite this, Kelli kept her voice calm. "All I'm saying is things might look up in the future. You have to look at the positive side of things. It might not be as bad as you think."

"How can you say that?" Nate spat back in rage.

Kelli stood to face him as her voice rose in annoyance. "God, Nate, would you just calm down for one moment?"

And that's when it happened. Even I didn't see it coming. How could either of them? One moment Nate was pacing back and forth, and the next thing I knew, he was yelling, "Shut up," and there was the sound of a slap ringing in my ears. Kelli had fallen to the bed. Her right hand held her face while her left was supporting her weight. The next moment, Nate was by her side apologizing.

"I'm so sorry, baby. I didn't mean it. I'm so sorry. Please forgive me. I need you right now." He put on a sad face and cuddled into her as if he was genuinely sorry.

Don't fall for it, Kelli, I thought, but the damage was already done. I was watching a scene that took place over a year ago.

Tears sprang to Kelli's eyes.

"Please don't cry, baby. I need you to be strong for me," Nate said.

"It's okay," Kelli said, stroking his hair. When she pulled her hand away from the point of impact, I could see a red hand-shaped imprint forming across her face.

What? How could she not see he was evil? Tears welled up in my own eyes, partially out of frustration and partially out of fear.

"I understand. You're going through a lot," Kelli told him.

The scene shifted again, pulling me back to the present. I didn't know how much time had passed, but Kelli was already off the floor, and the game was back in session. I stared at Kelli on the bench, a beautiful young blonde with a black eye that meant more to me than a volleyball injury. Someone had given her an ice pack, and she now pressed it to her eye. How could I help this poor girl? She'd comforted Nate in his time of need, but he never let her go.

I continued to stare at Kelli across the gym until a light figure formed in front of her. Olivia stood on the side of the court, her apparition barely visible under the gym lights. Her eyes found me in the crowd, and she mouthed those words again. "Help her!" And then she pointed a ghostly finger at Kelli.

CHAPTER 18

So it was all about Kelli, but what did Olivia know that Justine didn't?

I hadn't even noticed my mother staring at me, her eyes wide. "I know that look," she whispered under her breath, horrified. Mom wrapped an arm around me. I wasn't sure if it was because she was comforting me or because she wanted to get closer to whisper in my ear. "What's going on? You look like you've seen a ghost."

I couldn't answer. My body froze, paralyzed by what I'd just seen. My gaze locked on Kelli across the gym. I couldn't take my eyes off her. Nate had slapped her hard that first time, but what had he done since? How bad had it gotten?

I just nodded at my mother.

My mom shook her head. "No," she insisted. "It's more than that." She gently took a finger and turned my head toward her, forcing my eyes off Kelli to meet her gaze. "You will tell me about this later," she said sternly with the authoritative tone a mother is supposed to have yet one I hadn't heard in so long.

I nodded my head. I *had* to tell her. Now that I knew Olivia wanted me to help Kelli, I had to tell my mother.

Tears pricked at my eyes. I was both overwhelmed by my responsibilities as a psychic and fearful for Kelli. Would Nate hurt her when he drove her home from the game? How much longer could this go on? How bad did it really get?

Maybe I could tell Teddy about it and he could save Kelli. Why hadn't I paid more attention to Kelli before instead of being so selfish? If both Justine and Olivia came to me about their best friend, it had to mean this was serious.

The crowd burst into applause for the Varsity Hornet's final victory of the season. As people slowly began to descend the bleachers, I stayed put, still paralyzed in my spot. I could still see Kelli as Coach Kathy led her into her office. I guessed it was to check out her injury in privacy.

"Crystal, are you okay?" my mom said as she shook me a bit.

I nodded, but I couldn't speak.

She glanced back at Teddy, who was also looking at me. "We'll wait for you in the commons, okay?" she said. "Whenever you're ready."

I nodded again as a thank you for giving me my space. I stared at Coach Kathy's office and waited for Kelli to emerge. My mother and Teddy left me alone on the bleachers, but there were still fans chatting on the court, so I wasn't completely alone. I noticed volleyball players leaving the locker room from across the gym.

I wasn't sure what I was doing when I stood up and followed Kelli once she left the coaches' office. When I entered the locker room, it was silent. All the other players were gone, so it was just me and Kelli.

I heard a sob coming from behind the center row of lockers. I peeked my head around the corner to watch Kelli. She sat with her head down and gently touched the ice pack to her eye, which was swollen but not too bad. She sniffled. I wasn't sure if it was from the pain or because she had other issues going on.

"Hey," I said softly, coming around the lockers.

She jerked her head up at me in surprise but relaxed when she realized I was just another player.

"Hey," she greeted with a sniffle. "Am I in front of your locker?"

"No," I told her, sliding down onto the bench beside her. "I actually wanted to talk to you."

"Oh." She seemed disappointed. She clearly didn't want to talk to anyone.

"That girl on the other team really has a mean spike, doesn't she?" I said, trying to find some way to spark a conversation. Mostly, though, I didn't know what I was going to say to her.

Kelli let out a forced giggle. "Yeah, she does."

"Um... are you okay?"

"Yeah, I'll be fine. It's just a black eye. It's not like I've never been hit before." She hesitated. "You know, by a volleyball."

I gave her a sympathetic expression, yet my pulse quickened as I prepared for what I was going to say next. I wasn't entirely sure if it was smart to confront her with this, but I knew I had to try. "That's not really what I meant."

She glanced at me sideways and looked me up and down suspiciously.

I continued. "I mean, are you okay in general? Do you need help?"

Her expression shifted to suspicion, and her voice rose. "What are you getting at?"

I recoiled, pushing my way down the locker room bench

a bit farther for her benefit. I didn't want to appear overbearing, although I knew I'd already crossed the line. "It's just... some people aren't convinced that Nate is good for you." Before I could offer my help, she stood and cut me off.

"Some people? You mean Justine. I thought you two were talking about me that day in the locker room. Nate loves me. I don't know how Justine can't see that. Besides, what do *you* have to do with this anyway?"

I wanted to explain it to her, but I didn't think she'd believe me. Before I had the chance to say anything else, we heard the squeak of the locker room door and voices outside. We both looked toward the door, waiting for whoever just entered the room.

Justine emerged from around the lockers. Her gaze shifted from me to Kelli then back to me. I knew she was suspicious about what we'd been talking about, but she put on her best bubbly face to mask the awkwardness of the situation. "There you are Kelli," she said happily. "I've been looking for you. How's your eye?"

Justine walked past me to Kelli. I knew it was my cue to leave, but I stayed put.

"Some of the Varsity players are going out to celebrate. Are you coming?" Justine's question was directed toward Kelli, not to me even though my team had won our game as well.

Kelli took a few moments to answer. "I—I don't know. I guess I'll have to talk to Nate. He's my ride home."

"I can give you a ride home, Kelli," Justine offered.

Kelli shook her head. "Yeah, but Nate might get mad if I wander off without him."

Justine's tone grew angrier as they spoke about Nate. "God, Kelli, he doesn't have to be with you wherever you go, nor does he have to dictate when you are and aren't allowed to hang out with your friends."

Kelli hung her head, clearly aware of this fact yet too weak to fight it. "Let me just go to the bathroom, and then I'll ask him."

"You mean tell him," Justine corrected.

Once Kelli was in the bathroom, a separate room off the locker room, Justine spoke to me.

"Did you find something out?"

I shifted nervously. "Um... I know why he started hitting her."

"She *told* you?" Justine's voice was full of surprise. It was clear that Kelli never mentioned anything of the sort to her.

"No." I assured her. I lowered my voice. "I saw it. In a vision."

Justine cocked her head and studied my face to see if I was lying. She narrowed her eyes in thought. "You really are psychic, aren't you?"

I nodded because that was the only way I knew how to answer. The way she was quick to believe me rendered me speechless.

"What did you see?"

I lowered my voice to a whisper and told her quickly about how Nate became violent after his parents separated and how Kelli stayed to comfort him, but he never let her leave, and now he's obsessed.

"I knew most of that. There are even rumors that his mom tried to kill herself when it happened."

If she already knew all this, what was I doing here? What good were my visions if they didn't give us anything to work from?

"We need more than that," she insisted.

"Well, what do you want from me? No one is going to believe a psychic vision."

"I need you to find proof."

"But how?"

Before she could tell me, Kelli emerged from the bathroom.

Justine raised her voice so that Kelli could hear. She spoke casually as if we were speaking like this the whole time. "Yeah, the JV's invited too, so you should come celebrate with us."

"Yeah, maybe," I said, mirroring her casual tone. "But I'm really tired. I'll see you around."

I turned to leave. I wasn't out the door yet when I heard Kelli speak to Justine. "What is up with you hanging out with *her*?"

The door closed behind me before I heard Justine's response.

I was caught slightly off guard when I saw Nate standing against the wall near the locker room. He was watching for Kelli. His ominous eyes locked onto me for a moment, sending a wave of terror through my body.

"Crystal!" Emma squealed as she approached me with her arms wide open. I was thankful for this distraction. She pulled me into a tight embrace. "I've been looking for you. Did you see my awesome serves? Some of us are going out to celebrate. Do you want to come?"

"Isn't that what our pizza party tomorrow is for?"

Emma shrugged and grinned at me. "We can have pizza two times to celebrate for such a great season."

"I'm actually really exhausted. I'm going to go home and sleep."

"I wish you'd come, but I understand. See you tomorrow."

I found my mom and Teddy talking to other parents in

the commons and told my mom I was tired. I exchanged a glance of urgency with her, and she quickly rose from her seat and said goodbye to the other parents. Teddy followed.

Mom gave Teddy a kiss goodbye, and I waved as we split up in the parking lot when he left to go to his own apartment. Mom and I walked side by side back home but didn't speak.

When we finally got home, she spoke first. "Tell me what's up. I know that face. You saw a vision of something, and it scared you, didn't it?"

I didn't say anything for a long time. How could I not tell her? She had to know who Olivia wanted me to help. After contemplating how to tell her, I finally broke down and told her everything I knew.

My mom stroked my hair as I wrapped my arms around her waist. We were sitting in her bed after I had divulged all my secrets—and my anxiety about the responsibility—while she held me and I sobbed into her arms.

"Well, sweetie, we have these abilities so we can help people."

I sobbed. "I don't know if I want that type of responsibility. How am I supposed to help Kelli and get her away from Nate? Justine said she already talked to her and that Kelli won't say anything about him. Justine keeps insisting that I get some proof to save her, but how can I do that?"

"Well, if Olivia knows something, we'll figure it out tomorrow night. Now go get some sleep. You really need it."

I returned to my room without telling my mom that I didn't want to wait until tomorrow night to contact Olivia.

Maybe I could summon her myself, I thought, but that idea scared me. Truth be told, I didn't know *how.* She'd always come to me herself.

And then the realization of the obvious hit me like a ton

of bricks. Aside from the séance, Olivia only appeared to me when Kelli was around.

Only then did I realized something else. Olivia had come to me in a dream before. Maybe she would contact me tonight.

I fell asleep thinking about Olivia and hoping that would help me get in touch with her.

CHAPTER 19

They were fighting again. I can't stand the sound of them fighting. Fighting. Fighting. Always fighting.

I pressed my hands over my ears to block out the sound. "Stop," I begged, but my parents didn't hear me.

I looked toward my two brothers who were mimicking my actions. Tears were streaming down both of their faces.

"Look what you've done!" my mother yelled. "Now you've made them all cry."

"Me?" my father spat back. "You're the one always picking fights, Sarah."

"Please stop," I begged again, but my 8-year-old lungs didn't have the strength to make an impact over their screaming.

My mother's voice rang out over my own. "Well, if I could actually put an ounce of trust in you, maybe this family would start feeling like a family."

"Oh, please," my father spat back. "Like you do anything around here to make this place feel like a home."

My mother threw her hands up in the air and turned away from him. "I'm done. I can't handle this anymore."

"Don't you walk away from me!"

My father grabbed for my mother and pulled her back with all his force as his other hand smacked against her face. She sunk to the ground in defeat while he loomed over her in dominance.

My brothers' cries grew louder to mirror my own.

My father spun toward us with rage plastered on his face. "Nate, would you and your brothers just shut the fuck up?"

I was crying when I woke up and had to remind myself that it was just a dream. Those weren't *my* parents. I was okay. I was a bit disappointed that Olivia hadn't appeared to me that night. My mood lifted slightly when I replayed the dream in my mind and realized what it meant, that my abilities were giving me a glimpse into Nate's past. That meant another piece to the puzzle, albeit small.

I texted Emma that I wasn't going to meet her at our corner. Instead, I headed off to school early. Most people were already at school before I usually got there, so I had faith that Justine would be there early, too.

I arrived in the commons and scanned the tables. When my eyes found Justine, they locked onto her, willing her to look up and meet my gaze. Kelli and Nate were both sitting by her, and I wasn't about to ask her to talk with me privately in front of them. When she did look up, she noticed my stare almost instantly.

"Bathroom," I mouthed, and then I turned to go meet with her. When I opened the bathroom door, I was glad it was empty. I double checked the stalls this time just to make sure we were really alone.

Justine entered behind me. "Thank God. I've been dying to talk to you."

I told her about the dream I had about Nate.

"That explains a lot," she said, "but it's definitely no excuse."

"Justine," I said, really needing to get some questions off my chest. "What kind of proof do you expect me to find?"

She shrugged slowly while an apologetic expression fell across her face.

"Then what do you want from me?"

"Look," she said. "I don't know what proof there is, but I know there's something. Maybe a picture somewhere, but I've checked Kelli's phone and her computer, and I didn't find anything."

"How do you know there's something out there?"

"When I first caught on to what was happening and asked her about it, she got really defensive, almost angry, and then she said that I would have to go find the proof, like there was something out there."

"That's it?" I asked in disbelief. It didn't sound like much to go on. "And what if there isn't? Justine, why are we even playing this game? Why don't we just turn Nate in?"

She sighed. "You don't think I haven't thought of that? Crystal, Nate's mom works for the county court-house. She knows how to pull strings, and if there isn't any proof, then there isn't a case. Not to mention that I've tried everything to convince Kelli to leave him. What am I supposed to do if she doesn't want help?" Justine began pacing back and forth and ran her fingers through her long dark hair. I could see the tears welling up in her eyes. "God, I just want to help my friend, and she won't even let me. Crystal, you're my last hope to save her."

But where was I supposed to find proof? I couldn't just go snooping through Kelli's house. Besides, Justine already did that and didn't find anything. I wasn't entirely convinced there *was* any proof.

"Well, maybe she doesn't need saving if she doesn't want out," I suggested, but even as I said it, I didn't believe it.

"Believe me, Crystal, she wants out. She's just too scared."

I understood all too well. I was reminded of the way I felt her fear when Nate drove up in the car after practice. She couldn't admit what their relationship was like or he would hurt her even more.

I sighed. "I'll try my best to find proof. I'll focus harder, okay?"

"Thank you, Crystal," Justine said genuinely. She turned toward the door.

"Justine." I stopped her, wanting to ask the question that had been bugging me.

"Yeah?"

"How come you're so quick to believe in my abilities?"

She shrugged. "My grandma was psychic, and so is my aunt," she said casually as if being psychic was an everyday occurrence. And then she left.

I stared after her in disbelief. What? Justine came from a line of psychics? Could that mean that she was psychic, too? She couldn't be or she wouldn't be asking me for help, would she?

I exited the bathroom and found Emma and Derek in the commons just as the bell rang. We walked to our lockers together, but I stayed silent as I mulled everything over. There was possibly proof somewhere that could save Kelli. Justine might have some psychic abilities. And I still had to talk to Olivia tonight.

"I was reading up on the stuff we're doing tonight," Emma said at our lockers with a low voice. "And what I read said it works better if you have something from the person. Like something that belonged to them."

I eyed Emma suspiciously. What did she have in mind? "But we don't have anything," I pointed out.

"But we could get something," Emma suggested.

If we could get Kelli, I thought, *Olivia might actually make an appearance.* But I knew Kelli wouldn't go for it in a million years.

I still wasn't sure what Emma was getting at.

"Don't worry," she said. "I'll take care of it. I just have to get Derek to help me."

"You don't think what we're doing tonight is going to scare him off?"

She shook her head. "No. Besides, he'll help me either way."

How many more people would I let in on this secret? I wasn't just concerned about telling people about my abilities, but I was nervous about mentioning Kelli. Justine told me not to tell anyone about what was going on, but since Olivia was somehow involved, I had to tell the people at the séance about who we were supposed to help.

When I entered my first class, a blissful sensation washed over me. I knew that we would soon have our answers to everything.

CHAPTER 20

$\mathcal{I}$ set my volleyball jersey next to everyone else's on a table in the commons. After a victorious season, our coaches were rewarding us with a pizza party after school, which also doubled as turn-in-your-equipment-and-do-inventory day. Luckily, I got to enjoy pizza while our manager took care of inventory.

I gave Derek an apologetic look as he entered the gym with a stack of jerseys. *Sorry you have to do that, and sorry I've been such a crappy friend toward you lately,* I tried to say with my gaze. I really had been ignoring him, and even though I had a lot on my mind, I was excited to dress up with him tomorrow assuming tonight went well and Olivia helped us fill in the missing pieces to the puzzle that was Kelli and Nate's relationship.

Seventeen hungry girls gathered around the lunch tables as the coaches brought the pizza to us. I grabbed a piece of double cheese pizza and bit into it. It tasted like heaven. I moaned in pleasure and exchanged a glance with Emma to say I approved of the delicious meal. She widened her eyes back at me in agreement.

After just one slice, Emma bounced up from the table. "I'm going to go check on Derek, okay?"

"I'm sure he's fine," I assured her, and with the glance she threw back at me, I suddenly understood what was happening. This is what Emma was talking about earlier about having Derek help her. She was going to get Olivia's volleyball jersey from the storage room where Derek was returning the other jerseys.

I wondered if her jersey would even be in there. Surely her mom would have returned it to the school even after Olivia's death. It could have been anywhere when her room caught on fire, therefore not burning with her. I had heard that the house suffered little damage and that Olivia would have been fine if she didn't have asthma. Even if it was in the same room with her, would it have burned? Then again, most girls left their uniforms in their gym lockers. The school would have taken it back before they even gave the rest of her belongings to her family.

I didn't have to wonder about the jersey anymore because when I was enjoying my second slice of pizza, I watched Emma walk out of the gym and sneak down the hall toward her own locker. No one would have noticed the balled up jersey in her hand if they weren't looking for it, and no one did but me.

Emma sat back down as if nothing had happened and casually picked up another piece of pizza. People talked and laughed about the season. I joined in where appropriate, but my mind was once again stuck on more important subjects. I couldn't stop stealing glances at Kelli and wondering how I was going to help her. What was going to happen at the séance tonight, and how was I going to tell everyone about Kelli?

As I tried to sort out my thoughts, a wave of terror overcame me again. The blissful sensation I felt earlier disappeared. My vision clouded, and I felt woozy.

"Crystal, are you okay?" Emma asked. "You look terrible again."

My vision returned without any indication of why I was feeling the way I was. "Yeah, I'll be fine." I didn't believe my own words. All I knew was that I wanted to get away from the crowd so that I didn't embarrass myself if a vision was coming on. "I just need some fresh air."

"Want me to come with you?" she offered.

I glanced at her half-eaten piece of pizza and then at the other girls. Emma was having fun. I didn't want to worry her. "No, I'll be fine on my own."

I found my way outside and steadied myself against the side of the building. The air was thick, but a strong wind helped cool me down. I slid to the ground and closed my eyes as I focused on my breath to ease my anxiety. I knew something was coming, but I didn't know what to expect. Was Olivia somewhere nearby?

"I've been looking for you," a menacing voice said.

I opened my eyes to find a tall, muscular figure standing above me.

"Nate?" I asked in shock. "What are you doing here?"

"I'm here to pick up my girl."

I closed my eyes again. I didn't have the strength to deal with his crap.

"Did you hear me?" he snarled, crouching down to my level. He was dangerously close.

"No," I answered honestly.

"I said I've seen you talking to my girl again. I thought I told you to stay away."

"And what are you going to do if I don't?" I challenged, but I immediately regretted it. Even though I didn't think he'd actually carry out his threat, I was still undoubtedly scared of him.

"I'll make you pay."

I couldn't help but notice that he never made it clear *how* he would make me pay.

I was bold. I was *too* bold. Before I knew what I was saying, words escaped my mouth. "Well, if you don't leave Kelli alone, *I'll* make *you* pay."

He laughed. "A little girl like you? I'm so scared." Sarcasm dripped off his tongue.

I shook my head in disbelief and met his terrifying gaze. I didn't know where the courage came from, but I found myself saying, "You'd never go through with it. I'm not your girl, and I wouldn't put up with an asshole like you."

My own eyes widened in disbelief. I'd never swore at someone like that before. The words didn't feel like they were my own.

He recoiled, surprised that someone like me would stand up to him.

I took this opportunity to stand up. I turned away, prepared to get back to the commons where there would be witnesses. The clouds seemed darker than when I came outside, and the wind seemed to pick up.

Nate grabbed for me. He wanted the fight to continue, but as soon as his hand clamped around my wrist, a powerful gust of wind came crashing down on him. I caught a glimpse of a white figure. I watched Olivia's face twist in anger as her apparition lunged toward Nate, and he fell to the ground.

I took my chance and sprinted back toward the main doors while silently thanking Olivia for getting me out of there. I knew Nate wouldn't pursue a fight with witnesses around.

I steadied my breath as I returned to the table and replayed my own words back in my mind. I wondered if maybe the words I'd spoken *hadn't* been my own after all. I took one final calming breath. I was safe for now, but I still couldn't shake the feeling that this wasn't my last encounter with Nate.

CHAPTER 21

"What am I supposed to write?" I asked.

Even though I didn't invite Emma to stay the night, I was glad that she'd come over; otherwise I'd be all alone after our pizza party worrying about the rest of the night. On some level, I wanted to talk with Olivia *now*, but I was still nervous about doing it on my own.

Emma shrugged from where she sat on my bed. "Whatever comes to your mind. These exercises will help get us ready for the séance tonight."

Of course, we couldn't start until later, once Mom, Sophie, and Diane closed down shop, and since it was the night before the Halloween festival, I suspected they wouldn't be home until late, at which time we could finally bring our abilities together to contact Olivia. Since my mother had nothing to hide from me, we figured we could hold the séance at home. Despite my anxiety for tonight, I waited patiently and played along with Emma's games.

"How is this going to help me?" I cocked my head to the side and stared at her skeptically from my chair. I wasn't sure if she was serious about this exercise or if she was just avoiding our geometry homework.

"If we both write down three predictions, it will help us get in touch with our inner psychic."

"Okay, but what kind of predictions should I make?"

"Anything you want. The website said you should try making predictions for tomorrow, but I think you'll be fine with anything."

"Okay," I agreed reluctantly. "I'll try."

We both fell silent and bent over our pieces of paper. I closed my eyes and tried to get in touch with my "inner psychic." When nothing happened, I opened my eyes and stretched my fingers, then my neck, and then let my shoulders fall in relaxation. I closed my eyes again and reached toward a prediction.

I drifted as if I was no longer in my body. My mind wandered in a different realm. There was no sense of time there, just a peaceful ambiance that made me feel like I was floating. All of my thoughts left me as I found dominance over my consciousness. I didn't know how long I sat there.

"Those sound good." Emma's voice snapped me back into my body.

"What?" I asked, blinking up at her in confusion. She had moved from my bed and was now standing behind my chair at my desk.

"Your predictions," she said, pointing to my piece of paper.

I looked down to find words scrawled across the paper in my handwriting. I hadn't remembered writing anything.

"My predictions are probably just nonsense," Emma said, pushing her paper toward me.

I took it and read her predictions, admiring the perfect curves of her letters as I did so.

1. *I will fall in love within the year.*
2. *I will soon discover a food allergy I never knew about.*
3. *I will love pizza forever.*

"I just wrote that last one because I couldn't think of anything else more creative," she giggled as she took her paper back and bounced back to my bed to rewrite her predictions, which I knew weren't predictions at all. "This is really difficult and frustrating, though," she complained before she continued scribbling.

With Emma quiet, I took the opportunity to look at my own predictions. I stared down at my sloppy handwriting, took a deep breath, and read through them.

1. *The more answers you find, the more questions you'll ask.*
2. *Be patient with your heroic duties.*
3. *Put more faith in your friends. They might surprise you.*

"This is dumb," I complained to Emma. "These aren't even predictions. They're like cheesy things you would find in a fortune cookie."

Emma wrinkled her nose and stared at me seriously, blinking a few times. "You're kidding, right? Those are really good." She rose from the bed again and came to stand beside me to look over my shoulder at the choppy writing. "What do you mean by 'put more faith in your friends?' Are you lacking faith in me?"

I stared up at her nervously. Was I? I didn't really believe that she would magically turn psychic. Is that the kind of faith I was lacking?

To my surprise, she burst out laughing. It took me a few

moments to realize she was playing around with me. I laughed with her to ease my anxiety.

"I'm going to keep practicing," she said. "Your mom said that anyone can be psychic, so I'll probably take up meditation or something. Maybe we could start doing yoga together."

The doorbell rang and interrupted her. Emma and I exchanged a confused expression.

"Who could that be?" I asked. We were only expecting my mom and her friends, but they wouldn't have to ring the doorbell, and they wouldn't be home for another few hours.

I rose from my seat to get the door, but Emma grabbed my hand to stop me. "This is a perfect opportunity to practice," she said.

"Practice what?"

"Your psychic abilities. I read about this exercise where you try to guess who's calling or who's at the door. It can help you improve your abilities."

The doorbell rang again, but Emma wasn't going to let me go until I at least tried. I sighed and closed my eyes as I focused on the guest at my front door. It only took a few seconds before I saw an image of the mystery man, a guy my age with bright blue eyes and curly light brown hair.

I took off down the hall so that Derek wouldn't think I was trying to avoid him. Emma raced after me. I came to an abrupt halt at the front door and took a deep breath.

"Sorry, Emma, but your game is far too easy," I teased, opening the door.

Derek stood on the porch with his Cat in the Hat hat on. When he saw us, his face fell. "Aw, man, you guys are having a party without me?"

I giggled at him as he entered the house. I was excited that he was here. I wasn't sure if it was because we hadn't spent a lot of quality time together lately or if I was simply glad to escape Emma's games.

"Why are you wearing that?" Emma asked, pointing to his hat.

Derek shrugged. "I'm a sucker for Halloween. And I thought Crystal would find it funny, but I didn't expect to see you here, Emma."

"What brings you over?" I asked.

"I don't have to babysit my sisters tonight since Mom is home, so I thought I'd escape for a while. You don't mind, do you?"

Emma and I exchanged a glance. He couldn't stay, could he?

"Um… give us one minute," I said, pulling Emma back down the hall toward my bedroom. "He can't stay," I whispered once I closed my door. "I mean, something like a séance will scare him off, don't you think?"

"I don't know," Emma said, a hint of wonder in her voice. "He seems like he's taking the whole psychic thing pretty well."

"That's because he doesn't actually believe us. Look, I want to share this with him as much as you do, but we can't have a skeptic here when trying to contact Olivia. There's too much information we need, so I need as much time with her as I can get."

"Maybe we could—wait, what information?"

I sighed. I knew I had to tell Emma about Kelli sooner or later, but I figured it would be easier when everyone was together. "I'll tell you about it later. Are we going to get rid of him or not?"

"I think you should let him in on it. Your prediction said to put more trust in your friends."

She had me there, but was my prediction true? Did I need to put more faith in them?

"Look, Derek might be a skeptic, but he won't be if we can prove your talents to him. Come on," she said, grabbing my arm to lead me back into the living room. Ugh. More of her games? She had me feeling like a lab rat.

"Okay, Derek, you can stay," Emma told him when we came back into the room. "But on one condition."

Derek sat on the couch silently, but I could tell he was wondering what we were up to.

"We can't have any skeptics here tonight, so you either fully believe Crystal is psychic or you leave." Her tone was so demanding that I almost felt sorry for Derek.

Derek raised an eyebrow. "You guys are serious?"

We both nodded our heads.

"Look," Derek started, "the finding the pencil thing was pretty cool, but I don't know if I can really believe you're psychic, Crystal. I don't know what you guys are smoking."

That stung, but I didn't let it show. "If I'm not psychic," I retorted, "how did I know where to find Emma's copy of *Charlotte's Web*?"

Derek raised both eyebrows. "*You're* the one who told Emma where to find it?"

I nodded, but by his tone, I knew he still didn't believe me.

"I want to prove it to you, Derek," I said as I came closer and knelt beside him. "What can I do to prove to you what I am?"

He thought about this for a moment while Emma moved and sat on the couch next to Derek.

"What kind of pet did I have when I was four?"

I rolled my eyes at him. "First of all, it doesn't work on

demand like that. Second, I already knew you used to have a pet gold fish."

Derek snapped his fingers in disappointment and then stared me in the eyes. "I want to believe you, Crystal. I really do, but I don't know if I really believe in psychics."

I didn't know where it came from, but suddenly I was blurting out Derek's deepest, darkest secret that he hadn't told anyone about. "You're adopted."

My hand flew up to my mouth. Where had that come from? Was it even true?

Derek's eyes widened. "How did you—oh, my god. You are—you have to be. I mean, I just recently found out. My parents never told anyone. You—how long have you known?"

I looked at Emma for help, but her eyes were just as wide. Her jaw had practically fallen to the floor.

"I—I'm sorry," I said, shifting my weight and pulling my knees to my chest as my hands came up to cover my eyes. "I don't know how I knew. I didn't even know I knew. I just... I'm sorry. I didn't mean—mean to intrude."

Derek placed a hand on my shoulder to stop my babbling. He didn't say anything for a long time. None of us did. Then he bent down to my level and wrapped his arms around me. I felt warm in his embrace. He pulled my head to his chest and rocked me back and forth as Emma shifted her weight on the couch and came closer to stroke my hair. I was sobbing now.

"Crystal," Derek said, "don't cry. You don't have to cry."

"Please don't cry, Crystal," Emma sniffled. "Now I'm going to start crying."

When my sobs stopped, I released my hands and looked up at both of them. I wiped my eyes. "I'm sorry. I don't know why I'm so emotional. It's just, how can you trust me when I intrude on your personal lives like this? It's not fair to you."

Emma continued running her fingers through my hair. "It's okay, Crystal. We don't mind. Do we, Derek?"

Derek shook his head. "No, it's okay. I was going to tell you guys eventually. It's just that I only found out a few weeks ago. It was a bit of a shock."

As I looked back and forth between my two best friends, I realized how much we'd been hiding from each other. "No more hiding things," I told them, and they nodded back.

"Um… guys," Emma said after a few quiet moments. She looked down at her hands. "Derek, I'm sorry I didn't tell you, but my parents are getting divorced."

"Oh, Emma. I'm sorry. I'm sorry I didn't tell you guys I was adopted. I only found out when we went in to get my driver's permit, and they needed my birth certificate. My mom didn't want me to see it at first, but I looked at it anyway. I was just too surprised to say anything to you two, and it doesn't really change who I am."

"And I'm sorry I didn't tell you guys I was psychic sooner," I admitted. We all looked at each other and started laughing as if our problems were so trivial.

"Are you going to search for your birth parents?" Emma asked Derek after our laughter died down.

"No."

"Why not?" I asked.

"I guess the only reason I was put up for adoption was because my birth parents died. There's no one to go searching for."

"How did you end up with your parents?" Emma asked curiously, which put us on the subject of sharing our secrets for a long time.

I'd learned that Derek's parents thought they couldn't

have kids, so they were quite surprised when they found out they were pregnant with twin girls. I also found out he wasn't upset about being adopted or that his parents hadn't told him.

The conversation soon switched to Emma's parents' divorce. We were on the subject of my abilities, which Emma was raving about how cool they were, when the front door opened.

"What are you guys up to?" my mom asked as she entered, followed in toe by Sophie and Diane.

My best friends and I exchanged glances and burst out laughing again, reveling in our own little secrets.

Mom rolled her eyes at us. Then her expression shifted to nervousness. "Is Derek staying?"

I looked between my best friends as they did the same. "Well, Derek, are you staying?" I asked. What I was really asking was whether he believed me or not.

He shrugged. "I guess so. What are we doing?"

"We're holding a séance," Emma said casually.

Derek's jaw dropped to the floor.

CHAPTER 22

I was honestly surprised Derek was taking this so well. After he picked his jaw up off the floor, he seemed pretty cool with it.

We all sat around the kitchen table, the blinds successfully leaving us in privacy, the candles set around the table, and the number 17 volleyball jersey spread out in the middle. Everyone applauded Emma's efforts for getting the jersey, saying it was a good idea. I scolded her for stealing, but she promised she was going to return it.

My mother sat me at the head of the table. She said since I'd seen Olivia before, this was my thing, but I honestly didn't know how to run the show. I took a good look around the table to make sure everything was in place. Looking at the candles in front of me, I was reminded of the way Olivia died.

"Look, guys," I said, interrupting the chatter. "I have to tell you all something." Everyone stared at me expectantly, but I didn't know how to start speaking. I took a few breaths to gather my thoughts. "I know we're here for Olivia, but it's more than that." I kept my gaze low, not wanting to look anyone in the eyes. I had promised to keep this secret, hadn't I? But I knew they needed to know.

Sighing, I continued. "Olivia asked me to help someone, and I think that's why she's still stuck here. Her friend Kelli is in trouble, and I believe that if we contact Olivia, she'll help us help Kelli."

I looked up to meet their gazes. They were all still staring at me and listening intently.

"Kelli has been in an abusive relationship since before Olivia's death, and I think Olivia knew about it. That's the real reason we're here."

There. That wasn't too hard.

But I couldn't stop talking. I had more to explain. "Justine Hanson came to me to help Kelli, but I didn't know until yesterday that Olivia wanted me to help her, too. Justine is convinced that there's some proof out there. I don't know how. Maybe she's psychic, too."

Sophie scoffed.

"What?" I asked, looking up to meet her gaze.

She shook her head but spoke in a friendly tone. "Justine isn't psychic."

"How do you know? She said it runs in her family."

"And I'm part of her family." She pointed to herself proudly. Realization suddenly dawned on me. Sophie was the aunt Justine was talking about. How was it that I never knew they were related?

I didn't have time to wonder. I shook off this newfound information and focused on the real issue. "Regardless of how Justine knew, she claims that there's something out there that can help us save Kelli, and I think Olivia knows where it is."

I looked around again. They all seemed to understand. I

nodded, ready to get on with it and finally save the people I'd been sent to help. I looked back at the candles on the table, the ones that reminded me of how Olivia died. "Um, maybe we should get rid of the candles," I suggested. Everyone looked at me, but after a moment, they all completely understood. It just didn't seem right to have them lit when Olivia died because of a candle.

We blew out the candles and sat in total darkness—apart from the gentle illumination coming from the digital clock on the stove and the light from the street lamps seeping in past the curtains.

My mother sat opposite our oval table from me and explained how the séance would work. Even though you didn't need to link hands, we would hold hands to raise the energy in the room. She explained that we needed to set our minds free and to focus on Olivia. When she was done, it was my turn again.

"Um..." What exactly was I supposed to do? "Everyone link hands please."

I found Derek's and Emma's hands in the darkness. Once the circle was complete, I could feel the energy pulsing in the room.

I spoke gently. "I'd like for us to take a few moments to clear our minds. Forget about your troubles, be conscious of a wandering mind, and focus on Olivia."

It was completely silent for quite some time as I allowed everyone around the table to relax. I needed the time, too, so I cleared my mind and reached out toward Olivia. When I was ready, I finally spoke. "Olivia Owen, we know you want us to help Kelli, but we also want to help you. If you're here, we ask that you make your presence known."

We all waited, but nothing happened.

"Olivia, you came to me for help, and I'm ready to help

you. I want to help Kelli, too. What can you tell me about her? Olivia, please help us help you."

Still nothing. I continued by repeating several versions of my call out to Olivia, but I still couldn't get through to her. This routine seemed to last forever. I dropped my hands, which prompted everyone to open their eyes and look at me.

I stared back at each of them. "This isn't working."

Everyone exchanged glances, looking for someone to explain. Thoughts of self-doubt spun in my head. *Am I doing this right? Maybe I need more practice. What if I'm not strong enough?*

"What should we do?" Emma's voice cut through my thoughts.

No, I told myself. *I can do this. I believe in myself.*

That's when I realized that not everyone here did believe in me. I looked around the table nervously until my eyes fell upon Derek. All other eyes in the room followed.

Derek's face fell, and he nodded. "I get it."

"I am *so* sorry, Derek," I said. "It's just that we can't have a skeptic in the room."

He nodded again. His expression was one of apology. "I want to believe you, Crystal, but I guess I'm just not ready." He stood up. "I want to be here for you, though, no matter what I believe or what you're going through."

"I'm so sorry," I told him again.

"It's okay. Really. I'm the one who should be sorry. I'm screwing this whole thing up. You guys have fun, okay?" With that, he turned and left.

I wanted to follow him and make him understand, but I was more than ready to get in contact with Olivia. Olivia's need for me won out.

When I heard the front door close, I guided everyone

back to our séance. I linked hands with Diane and took a deep breath.

We sat in silence for several minutes. It was so quiet in the room that I swore I could hear each of our heart beats.

"Olivia," I called out again.

After a few minutes of focus, I felt a shift of energy in the room. A chill spread out from my spine to my fingertips. "Olivia! She's here!" I shouted the words. I wasn't sure if it was because of my own excitement or to inform the others. Even though I could feel her presence, I couldn't find a clear image of her. She was weak, it seemed, so I pushed further, reaching out to her and pulling her back into our realm.

"Olivia, we need your help to help Kelli. What can you tell us?"

Still nothing. After seeing her so easily and clearly the first few times, this almost seemed like too much of a struggle.

"Please, everyone," I begged, "clear your minds and focus on Olivia. She needs us to be strong for her."

With this reminder, suddenly the energy in the room shifted. I opened my eyes to search for her. Everyone else in the room still had their eyes closed. Had they not felt the energy shift?

"Olivia, come to us. We're here to help."

I could feel her reaching out to me, so I reached back.

"Crystal," I heard Olivia's voice in my head. "Help. Please help."

Shivers ran up and down my body.

"I'm—I'm not very strong," Olivia whispered in my head again. "I've become so weak after protecting you from Nate."

My hands gripped tighter around Diane's and Emma's. I wasn't sure if that had caused them to send the squeeze around the table and intensify our energy or if it broke something inside of me, but suddenly, the energy in the room burst like an ignited fire. I watched as a glowing Olivia appeared at the opposite end of the table next to my mother. Her blonde hair and brown eyes were bright in the dark room and clear as day.

Olivia rambled with urgency. "Crystal, I don't know how, but you can see me when no one else can. I need your help. I was going to help Kelli. I was, but I died before I got the chance."

"Slow down," I pleaded.

"I can't. I may not have much time. I never do. Please, just listen. You're the only one who can see me."

I nodded.

"The video. I left it in my locker. My mom. She has it. She kept it when they gave her back my stuff."

"Video, what video? And who gave her back your stuff?" I asked in as much urgency as she conveyed.

"I know I'm not making any sense." She stopped and thought for a brief moment. "Maybe this will help."

Suddenly, I was whipped from my seat at the table, spinning out of control, everything a muddle of confusion. I was falling fast until I came to an abrupt halt. My mind was still in panic mode, but my body seemed fine, comfortable in the situation even. However, I couldn't control my body, and when I finally focused on what I was seeing, I realized why. I was in one of Olivia's memories, seeing it through her eyes.

CHAPTER 23

I recognized the room I was in. It was vast, with a high ceiling and bleachers lining the walls. It smelled like sweat, dirt, and the familiar extras that came along with volleyball season. A volleyball net was set up in the center of the room. I was watching over it from the top of the bleachers. I could hear the hum of the ceiling fans and the thump of music coming from the coaches' office.

A lone girl stood at the back of the court. I watched as she tossed a ball in the air, jumped, and sent it flying across the net.

"Awesome!" I shouted, only it was Olivia's voice I heard. "I got that on camera, so we can study it later to see what you did right."

I looked over at the camera sitting on a tripod next to me. *Yep, the frame is perfect so that we see what's going on with her body. It won't take long until she has her jump serve down,* Olivia's thoughts said in her memory.

I looked back to the girl. The part of me that wasn't replaying the memory—the Crystal part—studied her face. I didn't recognize her at first, but then I realized it was Kelli, only she had darker hair and a rounder, younger face.

Kelli threw another ball in the air and jumped. It flew straight into the net. She turned in frustration to grab another one.

"That's okay," Olivia's voice assured her encouragingly. "That's why we stayed after practice to video tape it. We'll figure out what you're doing right and wrong."

Kelli jumped again, this time sending the ball flying crazy fast into the opposite side of the court. Kelli squealed in excitement and gave a hop for her success.

She grabbed another ball from the cart and stepped up to the serving line, but something caught her eye by the door. She did a double take.

"What are you doing here?" Kelli asked kindly before I even saw Nate storm into the gym.

"You better have a damned good excuse," he snarled, pointing at her. When he reached her, he seized the ball from her hands.

She recoiled, stunned by his anger.

I felt Olivia's body shift as she sprung up from her seat in alarm, but she didn't move down the bleachers.

"What are you talking about?" Kelli asked calmly. "I didn't know I needed to tell you I was staying after practice to work on my serves."

"Well, you should have. I've been waiting for you." Nate's voice was full of rage. He kept pointing his finger in her face. I didn't think he saw Olivia at the top of the bleachers looking down on them.

"I didn't know you'd come to pick me up. I usually walk home from practice."

"We talked about this. From now on, you ride with me."

"I don't think that's necessary." Kelli's voice was still calm.

I couldn't quite understand why, but Olivia stayed put. Her thoughts told me she was afraid this was something she shouldn't get into.

"Well, it is," Nate spat. "You don't get to hang out after practice when I'm expecting to spend time with you. You do as I say, okay?"

"No, I don't," Kelli said, crossing her arms over her chest and raising her voice to challenge him.

I didn't know how to react in my own mind or in Olivia's body.

"I want to work on my serves," Kelli said through clenched teeth as she snatched the ball back from his hands.

That's when it happened. A strong hand came up. Olivia bolted down the bleachers, but before she could get anywhere, I heard the loud smack against Kelli's face. She fell to the ground. Olivia continued racing toward her.

Nate looked up and saw me—well, Olivia—for the first time.

"You asshole!" Olivia shouted, but it felt like the words came from my own mouth even though I knew I would never be so bold as to stand up to him like that.

"You stay out of this," he barked back while pointing that ugly finger toward Olivia. She was still coming at him. She was so close now.

"You asshole," Olivia repeated, pushing him as hard as she could. I felt the impact in Olivia's memory.

He stumbled back a few steps. I knew she hadn't hurt him, only stunned him. Olivia bent to console her friend, but she didn't make it all the way down before Nate was pulling her back up.

"You think that's funny?" he spat. He shoved Olivia's body, sending her stumbling over her own feet, but she quickly regained her balance. He was advancing. "Kelli is *my* girl. You don't get to judge me."

"Oh, I think I can," Olivia's voice rang boldly. I applauded her bravery and then felt her body shift as she spoke again. "I thought you were a good guy, but Kelli deserves a lot better than this." Olivia stopped and folded her arms over her chest to show she wasn't afraid of him.

You go, Olivia, I thought as I experienced her past.

He paused inches away from her. "Better than me? She's never going to find anyone better than me. I'm all she's got."

"She's got me," Olivia challenged. "You lousy piece of shit."

He raised his hands, but before Olivia could duck out of the way, they came down on her, pushing her hard into the gymnasium wall. Pain shot through her back as her shoulder blade collided with the concrete. My own conscious mind felt a stab of pain, too. Olivia's hands came up to comfort her aching shoulder.

"*Nobody* says things like that to me," Nate snarled. "You best remember that, bitch."

He turned away like nothing had happened. "Get off the floor," he mumbled to Kelli, and to my amazement, she rose and followed him. Before she left, she sent Olivia a look of apology.

I have to go after him, Olivia thought in my mind. She started toward them. Kelli shook her head like it was just better if Olivia stayed. *That's fine,* her thoughts said in my mind. *I have a video of his violence, and Coach Kathy is in her office. We'll be okay.*

I expected the memory to end there, but it didn't. Still watching from inside Olivia's memories, she returned to her camera at the top of the bleachers and stopped the video before packing up her equipment. She took special care of her camera as she placed it in her bag, and then she walked slowly back down the bleachers while both of our minds tried processing what had just happened. Olivia glanced up only to see the opposite end of the gym covered in stray volleyballs.

She set down her camera and grabbed the cart, pulling it to the opposite end of the court to collect the balls. I could feel that she needed something to calm herself down before she told Coach about Nate. When she had all the balls picked up, she returned the cart to the storage room and went to retrieve her camera equipment.

Loud music was still coming from the coach's office, so Olivia pounded hard on the door. Coach Kathy still didn't hear, so Olivia turned the knob and entered. Coach looked up from her paperwork, smiled, and spun her chair toward her radio and turned it off.

"You girls all done? You don't have to put the net away because the gym teacher asked us to keep it up for badminton."

"Actually, Coach, I was really hoping to talk to you about something," Olivia said.

Coach sat back in her chair to listen.

"About what? How are Kelli's serves coming along?"

"Pretty good, but I really need to talk to you about something else," Olivia said again. "About Nate and Kelli."

"And?" she prompted.

Olivia didn't know how to say it. "It's just... Nate's done something really bad, and I'm scared for Kelli."

"Nate Williams? No. He's a good kid."

I should have known, Olivia's thoughts said in my mind. *Coach is friends with his mom. She wouldn't hear any of this.* But Olivia tried anyway. "No, I'm serious. You have to watch this video."

"Look," Coach said, "I've known Nate and his family for a long time. Whatever happened, I'm sure there's been some misunderstanding. Nate's a good kid."

"But he's *not*," Olivia insisted.

She wouldn't have any of that. "The janitors will lock everything up. I trust you can find your own way out."

Olivia stared at her, stunned. *I don't get it. Does she just not want to believe he's bad? Does she think I'm too young to understand?*

Olivia carried herself back to her gym locker in disappointment and slowly changed out of her practice clothes and into her street clothes. She glanced into the mirror to assess her injuries. Nothing. She shoved the camera into her locker, intent on showing another authority figure—maybe the principal?—the next day at school.

As soon as she slammed the locker, my mind was falling again out of Olivia's memory. I fell hard back into my own kitchen.

CHAPTER 24

Olivia was still standing in front of me. My jaw dropped. Holy crap. There really was proof that would help save Kelli.

"Where is it?" I insisted in urgency, staring into Olivia's brown eyes. Then she showed me something again, but this time it wasn't as fierce of a transformation.

Instead, she sent me floating through town until I came above her house. I could tell which room was hers because that was the part of the house with new shingles. I floated down through her ceiling until I felt like I was standing on solid ground. It didn't look like a girl's room anymore. There wasn't a bed. Instead, it was full of boxes. Her mother had turned her daughter's old room into a storage room.

Olivia continued leading me until I moved to the boxes. I could see into them, and I knew exactly which box the video camera was in. When I had this information, Olivia pulled me back.

"I lit a candle that night to pray for her," Olivia admitted in a quiet voice. "I didn't know it would be the last prayer I ever made."

My heart ached thinking about what she'd been through.

"My mom saved all my stuff, but she packed them away. The school gave her back the stuff in my locker, and she just tucked that away with everything else. She never saw the video, but now you can. You can save Kelli."

"I will," I promised.

Olivia looked at me with grateful eyes. "Thank you so much, Crystal," she said, and then she faded, the energy in the room washing away with her. Everything went dark again.

I released my hands from Emma's and Diane's, which caused everyone to open their eyes and look at me. "She's gone," I announced. "I—I don't know if she crossed over, but I can help Kelli now."

My mom rose and flipped on the light. "What happened?"

"You mean, none of you saw her?"

They all stared at me and shook their heads in unison.

"But she was standing right there." I pointed to the spot across the table where she had stood.

"Crystal," my mom explained. "You're the only medium here. We can hear spirits, but none of us can see them."

"All I heard was Crystal," Emma interjected but spoke softly in wonder. "It was like a one-way conversation."

My mother nodded in thought. "That makes sense since this is your first time and you don't have much of a connection to the other side." My mom turned back toward me. "I didn't hear Olivia say much, though. She must have shown you something."

I sat there completely stunned for what seemed like forever. From the seat next to me, a giant smile formed across Emma's face.

"This. Is. So. Cool!" Emma exclaimed.

I offered a shy smile because I wasn't entirely certain. Seeing dead people? Did I really want that? Emma seemed to want it more than I did, but it didn't matter what I wanted right now. I had the information I needed. After I took a few breaths to calm myself, I told them everything I knew.

"Do you guys think this is the right thing to do?" I asked warily. "I mean, I saw Nate hit Kelli. It was in a vision, but still. Couldn't we just turn him in?" I was instantly reminded of what Justine had said. She'd told me that she tried to turn him in, but without any proof, there was nothing they could do. But what was I even doing? What if Kelli didn't want help? Somewhere deep inside of me, I knew that she did by the way she was overcome with fear when he picked her up that day after volleyball practice. I wasn't even sure there would be a case against him if Kelli didn't want that, but maybe Justine could convince her otherwise.

All this went through my head in a few moments. My mother's words snapped me out of my thoughts. "This is what Justine asked you to do, isn't it?"

"Yeah."

"Then I think you need to stick with it," she said, and I knew she was right.

Now that I had answers, I only had more questions. How was I going to get it? What would I do with the video when I found it?

Emma spoke next. "Well, let's go get it."

"What? Now?"

"Yeah," Emma said. "It's only, like, nine. It's not that late."

I figured it wouldn't hurt, and we were only a few blocks away. "Okay," I agreed.

Emma and I found Derek sitting on my front steps.

"How'd it go?" he asked.

I thought about this for a moment. "Really well, actually."

"I'd still like to help if I can," he offered.

Several minutes later, Emma, Derek, and I were walking through the streets in the dark, led only by street lamps. My mom, Sophie, and Diane stayed back. They said this was my problem to deal with. I'd have been more comfortable with an adult coming along, but I had a feeling they were trying to teach me something.

I explained things to Derek as we walked.

I knew the house when I reached it, not just from the dream, but because in a town like this, you know who lives where. I walked up the porch steps and rang the doorbell. My best friends remained safely behind me. It took a few moments, but then I heard motion behind the door, and the porch light turned on.

Tammy Owen opened the door. She was wrapped in a robe and slippers. Her blonde hair was wet, and she was makeup free like she'd just taken a shower.

"Um. Hi, Mrs. Owen," I greeted nervously. She stared expectantly behind the screen door, so I continued, not quite sure what to say. Crap. Why didn't we come up with something good to say?

"Hi," she greeted with a smile. "You're Andrea Frost's daughter, aren't you?"

"Yeah, I'm Crystal, and these are my friends." I gestured to Emma and Derek. "I'm sorry it's so late, but we're looking for something really important."

"I'm not sure if I can help you."

"It's about Kelli Taylor."

"She was Olivia's friend. What about her?"

"Well, I think you have something that could really help her."

"Why?" Mrs. Owen asked seriously. "Is Kelli in trouble?"

I glanced back at Emma and Derek for help then turned back to Mrs. Owen. "Sort of. We were really hoping we could go through Olivia's boxes to find it."

She didn't wait for a further explanation but rather crossed her arms over her chest and glared at us. "No. I hardly know you. If Kelli needs something, she can come and get it herself." She reached for the door.

"Wait," I called, but the door slammed, and the porch light went out. I whirled around to glare at my friends. "Why didn't you guys back me up?"

They both gave surprised expressions.

"I'm sorry," Derek said.

"We didn't know what else to say," Emma apologized at the same time.

I pushed past them down the stairs and started walking back toward my house. What was I thinking? How could I think she would just let me dig through her boxes?

The only other possible way I could think to get the video was to get Justine to ask Tammy for it. Surely Tammy was still on good enough terms with Justine, one of Olivia's best friends.

"I feel like I should call Justine and tell her about everything we found out," I confided in my friends as we walked. "I think she might be able to help us get the video, but I don't even have her number."

Emma's face lit up as pulled her phone out of her pocket. "I do."

"What? How did you get her number?"

She shrugged. "When I got my new phone, it put in all my Facebook friends' contact numbers."

"Oh, you're friends with Justine?"

"I'm friends with practically everyone on the volleyball

team. Here you go," Emma said, holding her phone out to me.

I took it and hit the call button. I knew it was getting late, but it was also a Friday night, so I suspected Justine wasn't asleep yet. She seemed wide awake when she answered.

"Hello?"

"Justine? This is Crystal Frost."

"Oh, uh. Hi, Crystal. Do you have anything new?"

"Yeah, I have lots. I know where your proof is, but my friends and I still need your help."

"Your friends?" she squeaked into the receiver. "I told you not to tell anyone!"

"It's okay, Justine. They helped me find the proof."

That seemed to make it okay with her, and she calmed down. "That's great news, Crystal. Do you have it?"

I bit my lip nervously. "Not yet. I was hoping you could help us get it. We need someone like you who Tammy can trust."

"Tammy Owen?" Justine's voice wavered a bit. "You mean, the proof is at her house?"

"Yeah. It's in Olivia's bedroom."

Justine hesitated. "You have no idea how much I want to help you, Crystal, but I don't think I can go there. Not after what happened to Olivia in that room. I haven't even been able to pass her house since it happened. Look, I trust you. Do you think you can get it without my help?"

My heart froze in my chest. In my mind, I was thinking, *No, no I don't think I can.*

"I want to help Kelli more than anyone," Justine said. "If you don't think you can do it without my help, maybe I can—"

"No," I cut her off. I couldn't force that upon her. I knew exactly how she felt. I still avoided the intersection where my dad died. If someone had tried to make me go back there... I couldn't finish that thought.

"Um, just one sec." I placed my hand over the receiver and spoke quietly to my friends as we walked. "She says she can't face the place of Olivia's death. What are we going to do now?"

They were both silent for a few seconds as if thinking, and then Emma spoke. "There's only one more thing we can do."

"Yeah. Turn him in," I suggested.

"No," Emma continued. "We could steal it."

"What?" I squeaked and looked at her in disbelief.

Derek was giving her the same expression.

"Stealing? No. I don't steal," I said.

"But it's so perfect," Emma insisted. "Tammy will be at the Halloween festival tomorrow night, so her house will be empty. You said you know where it is. We can get in and out of there in a matter of minutes."

"She does have a point," Derek agreed, and I gawked at him, unable to believe that he was considering this.

"You guys have got to be kidding me. I don't steal things, and I certainly don't break in."

"Since no one locks their houses around here, it's technically not breaking in," Derek pointed out.

I stared back at them in skepticism. What else could I do, though? This was my responsibility, wasn't it?

I sighed. "Fine. But someone needs to be at the festival to keep an eye on her, okay? I don't want anyone catching us." I looked between them both and wondered who would volunteer.

Derek raised his hand. "Okay, I'll keep watch. You two can do the sneaking. If I notice anything, I'll text Emma."

My mind continued to contemplate the ethics of this

decision. How did I get dragged into this, and why was getting ahold of a video the best solution? It didn't make any sense to me.

I sighed and brought the phone back up to my face. "Justine, I'll get it for you."

She squealed excitedly into the receiver. "Thank you! When can you get it to me?"

"You'll be at the festival, right? I can give it to you then."

"Yeah, I'll be there. I'm helping out with some of the booths, so if you walk around, you'll probably see me. I'll be in a butterfly costume. I can't wait! We're finally going to get him, and I'll have my best friend back!"

Her excitement was palpable. It made me feel great that I was able to help, which for the first time since she'd asked me for help made me feel welcoming about my abilities.

"I'll see you tomorrow," Justine said, signaling the end of our conversation.

"Wait," I said, stopping her.

"Yeah?"

"What are you going to do with the video?" I asked.

"It's a video!" She seemed even more amazed. "Wow. You really are a good detective, Crystal. You know what I'm going to do with it? I'm going to use it to send the piece of crap to jail."

I wasn't sure if that was even possible, but even so, I figured it would help to at least get Kelli out of the relationship. Maybe Justine and Kelli could use it as blackmail against Nate.

"Thank you so much, Crystal. Seriously."

"I'm glad I could help."

I hit the end call button and handed Emma back her phone.

Emma and I said goodbye to Derek when we got back

home. We found the fold-up cot and set it up in my room next to my twin bed. Emma and I lay side by side facing each other and talking about the situation we were in.

I was feeling better that this was almost all over, but when my head hit the pillow, I reminded myself that I still had to break into someone else's home. That sent a sickening sensation throughout my body.

CHAPTER 25

*E*mma and I couldn't sit around with nothing to do all day, so we tagged along with my mom to help with the festival. My mom didn't mention anything about our adventure. I didn't think it was because she didn't care but rather because she was so busy.

I wondered why Emma and I couldn't just go to Tammy Owen's house now. She had to be here somewhere, right? When I spotted her, I understood why it was a good idea to wait. I watched as she hopped into her car and announced to a few other helpers that she had to pick up more supplies from her house. I didn't know how many trips she was going to take, but I didn't want to risk the chance of her catching us.

Emma and I spent most of the morning helping set up tents at the park, moving around supplies, and decorating. Some people from the community brought all the workers sandwiches for lunch, and Emma and I sat by the creek as we ate. We didn't talk about our plans for that night or being psychic because we didn't want anyone to overhear, so we kept our conversation casual.

As we put up more decorations and more people showed up to set up their booths, the Halloween festival really started looking amazing. There was my mother's tent for fortune telling, some carnival games, food vendors, apple bobbing, a kissing booth, and even a huge stage for a band.

Around three o'clock, Sheryl tested the microphone on stage and began barking last-minute orders since we only had an hour until the festival officially started.

"Why aren't you girls dressed yet?" I heard a familiar voice behind me and turned to see my mother with caked-on makeup, curly hair, gaudy jewelry, and flowing clothes. She really had the gypsy look down.

"We don't have our costumes with us," I said.

"Well, go get them! I don't want to be the only one dressed up. Here, take my car." To my surprise, my mom put the keys in Emma's hands. Of course, I didn't have my license, so she certainly wasn't going to let me drive.

"Awesome," Emma said, pulling at me. "Let's go get our costumes. See you later, Andrea."

As we were walking back to the parking lot, we spotted Derek coming our way in his own costume.

"You guys are leaving already?" he joked as he approached us.

"We're just going to get our costumes," Emma answered, "but we might not be back for a while."

"Okay. I'll keep you updated."

As soon as we walked away from Derek, I saw a tall girl with dark hair and wings trailing behind her. She was coming toward us.

"Do you have it?" Justine asked when she was close enough.

"We're going to get it right now," I answered, excited that this was all working out.

"That's great. I can't wait." Then to my surprise, Justine bent down—she was a lot taller than me, especially with her heels on—to embrace me. "I'd come with you, but I promised I'd help run the kissing booth for the first shift." She pulled away. "And Crystal, I'm really sorry about blackmailing you. I wasn't actually going to tell anyone your secret. I just really needed your help."

I smiled in forgiveness and thanked her, but her last words echoed in my mind. "Justine, if you have psychics in your family, why didn't you go to them about this? Why me?"

Justine gave me a look of apology like she was sorry she dragged me into this. "From everything I know about my family's gift, it's not very strong. And my aunt is only an empath, after all. It just sounded like you had a gift that could honestly help in this situation." She paused. "I was right, wasn't I?"

I smiled and realized that yes, I think she was right.

Emma and I said goodbye and made it to the car. Emma climbed in behind the wheel while I found my place in my usual seat. I pulled out my phone from my pocket and texted Derek.

Have you spotted her yet?

No. Someone said she was picking up a few last-minute things at home.

Crap. Okay. Thanks.

"We can't go get it yet. Tammy's at home," I told Emma.

"Okay, so we'll stake out by her house."

I shook my head. "I don't know. I think she'll notice and suspect something. She knows my mom's car, which is supposed to be at the park."

"You're right. Maybe we should just go get our costumes first."

"Yeah, I guess we can do that."

So we went to my house instead and slipped on our red onesies, which were surprisingly comfortable.

"I think we can leave these in the car when we rob Tammy Owen's house," I suggested, rolling my blue pompon wig in my hand.

"Crystal, it's not robbing," Emma said as she adjusted her own wig. "It's Olivia's camera, and she wants us to have it."

I thought about that for a moment. "Yeah, I guess you're right." The familiar chime of my phone sent me reaching for it.

I've spotted her. You're good to go.

Awesome. Thank you, Derek.

BTW, I thought I was supposed to be texting Emma.

She's my driver.

Lol. Ok. Good luck.

"Okay, we're good to go," I told Emma.

"Sounds good. Ready for your first criminal act?"

I rolled my eyes at her. "According to you and Derek, we're not breaking and entering or stealing, so I think we're good."

Emma laughed as we headed back to the car. The sun had fallen low in the sky, but it still wasn't dark.

"Do you think anyone's going to suspect anything?" I asked warily.

"No. First, a lot of people are at the festival. Second, we'd just look like we were sent to pick up supplies or something. No one is going to see us. We'll be fine."

"Even in these?" I gestured toward our costumes.

"People will just think we've been downtown." She had a point.

It didn't take long to make it to Tammy's house. We parked across the street and looked around to make sure no one was watching. We couldn't see anyone, but the hairs on the back of my neck still stood as if someone *was* watching us.

I scanned the street again. No one. *I'm just nervous*, I told myself until I believed it.

"Okay, I think we're set to go." My heart pounded as I took off my seat belt and opened my door. Even though the air was cool, I felt almost too warm in my costume, which made me sweat all over.

"Well, *are* you ready?" Emma stared at me as I simply stood there, but when I nodded, she took my arm and led me across the street.

I wasn't even surprised when the back door opened easily. We walked onto a landing where one set of stairs led to the main floor and the other to the basement. I climbed the stairs and found myself in a pristine kitchen. I led the way, although I wasn't entirely sure the layout of the house.

"Her bedroom is upstairs," I whispered, even though I was sure we were alone. "Stay quiet."

"Why?" Emma asked, mirroring my volume.

"I don't know. I just feel better about it. The stairs are over here." I rounded a corner and went down a hallway before I crept up the stairs. I was careful not to make a sound. When we came around the banister, the door I was looking for was already open.

And then I heard it, which only made me creep back down the stairs and hide. I gripped the owl pendant that hung around my neck and rubbed it for good luck. I peeked up to the floor's level to try to see into the room, but I couldn't tell what was going on.

"Text Derek," I mouthed to Emma. I handed her my phone after making sure it was on silent.

I watched intently, trying to detect what was happening in the room. It sounded like someone was shuffling through boxes. I heard footsteps, and then objects shifted as they bounced against each other in their containers. I listened closely and heard rapid breathing and then a sob.

"Derek says she's still there," Emma whispered so quietly that even I could hardly hear her. Then who was digging through boxes in Olivia's room?

I snuck back up the stairs, intent on finding out who was screwing up our operation. My pulse quickened as I thought about the possibility of getting caught. I pressed my body against the wall as I slowly and quietly stepped closer to the room. Then even slower, I peeked around the open door. I could feel Emma right behind me.

A young woman about my age with blonde hair was facing away from me and shuffling through boxes. She was dressed in a baby blue dress, white tights, and black flats.

"Where is it?" she mumbled, lightly kicking one of the boxes in frustration. I knew who it was immediately.

Without thinking, I emerged from my hiding spot and entered the room. "Kelli, what are you doing here?"

CHAPTER 26

elli Taylor whirled around to face me. "Me? What are *you* doing here? And in your pajamas?"

My pajamas? I looked down at my costume. I liked our Cat in the Hat idea. I liked her Alice in Wonderland costume, too, but this was no time to admire costumes.

"Um... Tammy sent Emma and me to get something for the Halloween festival." At the mention of her name, Emma came into the room. "We heard something up here and thought you were a burglar or something." I could feel my eyebrow twitching.

I was never good at lying, so I was shocked when Kelli bought it. I released the tension in my shoulders.

"Me?" she said. "No, not a burglar. I'm just looking for something."

Emma, knowing I'd never been a good liar, took over for me. "Tammy sent us for something in the boxes, too, so do you mind if we look with you, do you?"

Kelli scowled. I wasn't entirely sure she believed us

anymore. "But this is all Olivia's stuff."

"And apparently yours," Emma said casually as she went over to a box and flipped it open to peer inside.

Kelli had shifted boxes all over the room so that it didn't look quite the same as when Olivia showed me where the camera was. Yet somehow, I still knew where it was as if its energy drew me closer. Suddenly, I understood what energy I was feeling.

Olivia's spirit sat above the boxes and peered down at me. I thought I'd helped her cross over, but she wasn't gone yet. I briefly wondered how she'd appeared so easily and why I wasn't feeling as woozy as I normally did when she appeared. As I thought this, she glanced over at Kelli, and I realized why. Her connection with Kelli was strong enough to ground her here if she was close enough.

"Tell her," Olivia said from her perch, although only I could hear her.

"What?" I asked. Both Kelli and Emma stared at me.

"Crystal, are you okay?" Emma asked.

"Tell her where it is," Olivia repeated.

"Yeah, I'm okay Emma, but why?"

Kelli and Emma both gave me a weird look again.

"Look," Kelli said. "I don't know what you guys want, but you're not going to find it here. These boxes are all full of Olivia's stuff."

"You have to show it to her," Olivia told me.

As much as I didn't think that was a good idea, I figured Olivia knew better than me. I sighed and moved aside several boxes until I found the one I was looking for. I pulled it free, set it on the floor, and opened it.

Inside was the same camera case Olivia was carrying in her memory along with her tripod and other belongings I didn't recognize. I pulled the bag from the box and stood up.

"Is this what you're looking for?" I asked, holding it out to Kelli.

"Oh, my god, yes!" she exclaimed while reaching out for it.

"Crystal," Emma scolded in the same moment. "What are you doing?"

"No!" Olivia cried, which made me recoil. I pulled the camera bag back to my chest. "Don't give it to her. Show her the video. She has to see it."

"Just hold on," I said, trying to calm everyone, including myself. I unzipped the bag, and Kelli watched wide-eyed.

"That's mine! You can't do that." Kelli lunged toward me, but Emma stepped in between us to stop her.

"Actually," I said, "I know for a fact this was Olivia's." I pulled the camera from the case. It was a large digital camera, clearly made for a photography lover. I pushed the power button, but it didn't turn on.

"There's a fresh battery in the front pocket," Olivia told me.

I continued talking to keep Kelli at a safe distance while I retrieved and changed the battery. "For one, Olivia was the photographer, not you. Only she would own a camera this expensive." I didn't know how I knew it. The words simply flowed from my mouth. I wasn't sure whether they were true or not, but I suspected they were by the way Kelli simply stood there and listened. "Not to mention that the strap has her initials on it. But the real proof is on the camera, isn't it, Kelli?"

I had the batteries changed by now. This time when I pressed the power button, it turned on. The battery wasn't full, but it was enough to do what I needed.

"And what do you think is on it?" Kelli asked accusingly.

"I don't know," I replied innocently, even though I did know. "Why don't we see?"

I pressed the playback button. The video I was looking for was the first image to appear. I pressed the play button, initiating the sound.

"You don't know what you're doing! Give that here!" Kelli dove for me again, but Emma came to my rescue for a second time and caught her before she could get very far. They were both stronger than they looked, but Emma was bigger and could hold Kelli back.

"Kelli, we're only here to help you," I said evenly, hoping my tone would calm her down. The video was playing through her serves. I knew we didn't have much time until Nate would walk into the gym and slap her. "Kelli, your friends are worried about you, both Justine and Olivia, and they asked us to help. Now, I want you to take a look at this. If you can honestly tell me that you're okay with what Nate has been doing to you, we'll let you go, and I won't intervene anymore."

"What is it with you?" Kelli asked. "You and Justine really are plotting against me, aren't you? Nate's not a bad guy."

"Really?" I asked, knowing full well the video was almost at the point where he came in. "This doesn't look that bad?"

I turned the camera so that she could watch the video play back. I listened as Olivia's memory replayed itself on the screen. I watched Kelli's face fall as she stared at it.

"You better have a damned good excuse," I heard Nate say through the speaker, but I was watching Kelli. Tears sprang to her eyes. Her bottom lip quivered as she watched. And then the sound of skin on skin, Nate slapping Kelli, came through the small speaker on the side of the camera, which only caused Kelli to fall to the ground. I wanted to pull the camera away, but when I looked toward Olivia for guidance, her eyes told me to keep the video playing. I didn't drop the camera, and Kelli didn't avert her gaze. She continued watching until the thud came, the one when Nate shoved Olivia into the wall.

"Okay, okay. Stop it!" she shouted in tears.

I felt awful, like I was the one torturing Kelli now. I turned the camera around and stopped the video. I removed the memory card and placed the camera back in the bag.

Kelli curled up on the floor, knees to her chest and face in her hands. Nobody said anything for a long time until Kelli's croaked voice broke the silence. "I—I never thought it was that bad, but seeing it from a different angle... Oh, my god. He hurt my friend, my best friend."

"I know, Kelli." I aimed for a comforting tone as I bent down to her level.

"I was going to destroy the video. When Justine said she had proof to help me, that she was going to get a video tonight, I knew the video she was talking about, only I didn't think it still existed. I thought it'd burned in the fire."

That explained why she was here now and why she was in costume. She must have just found out after we told Justine we were going to get the video now, only since we'd waited for Tammy to leave, Kelli got here first.

Kelli sobbed again. "I—I never intended to watch it, but... it's just so horrible. I thought I loved him, you know. I mean, I do. I do love him, but he can just be horrible sometimes."

"I know, Kelli. That's why you have to turn him in. You shouldn't have to live with this, and neither should your friends." I took a gamble and rubbed her shoulder. To my surprise, she didn't pull away.

"No, they shouldn't, but what if he hurts me if I turn him in? He'll come after me." She looked up at me, her eyes glistening with tears. "I was lucky enough to get away from him tonight for the festival. He didn't want to come. If I had ditched him there, he'd have my head on a silver platter. But it'd be my fault, you know. It always is. I shouldn't be here without him." Kelli started to get up. "I should go to him. We should destroy the video. That's what Nate would want. "

"Kelli," I said kindly. "You can make your own choices. Nate doesn't have to dictate everything you do." I found myself repeating Justine's words and feeling a deep sense of truth to them.

She shook her head. "You don't understand."

"There are people who can protect you, Kelli," Emma said. "Besides, you have friends to help you."

"I know. Nate is good to me most of the time, though." She paused. "I have Justine, but Olivia was always my true best friend, and—and when she died, I was so screwed up. Nate was there for me through it, you know? How could I leave him then? And now—now how can I leave him?" She lowered her voice to a whisper. "I've been so terrified the past year that if I leave him, he'll not just go after me, but he'll go after my family and friends. I mean, look what he did to Olivia over something so stupid."

She took a deep breath. "I thought about leaving him this summer," she admitted. "I found out I was pregnant, only when I told him, he freaked. I lost the baby."

Emma and I both drew in a quick breath. I was reminded about something Justine said. *It's like something happened between them last summer.*

"I don't know why I'm even telling you this. I never told anyone. But I can't just *leave* him. I love him and hate him at the same time. You two wouldn't understand."

"Kelli," I tried. "You're not in this alone. You have to admit it to your family and friends, and they can help you. Maybe one of them will understand better than us."

She nodded and sank to the floor again. After a few breaths, she looked at us. "How did you guys get roped into this? I mean, why didn't Justine just do it herself?"

I exchanged a glance with Emma. "Justine doesn't exactly know what happened yet," I admitted.

"Then how do you?"

I contemplated this for a moment, wondering if I should tell her. I glanced back at Olivia on her perch, but she wasn't there anymore. I turned my head back toward Kelli and nearly jumped out of my skin when I saw Olivia standing behind her. Olivia nodded as if to say it was okay to tell Kelli.

"I know because Olivia told me."

"She told you? But you hardly ever talked to her."

"You're right. I didn't really talk to her when she was alive."

Kelli's eyes skimmed over me. They still sparkled with tears. "What are you getting at?"

"Kelli, I've talked to Olivia recently. She's the one who told me that the video was still here."

"What?" she gasped. "Like, you talked to her ghost?"

I took a deep breath. "Yes, and she's here right now."

Kelli's sorrow turned to rage. "Whatever sick joke you're playing, it's not funny. Olivia is dead."

"I'm not joking," I defended.

"Well, if she's really here, then ask her what gift I got her the Christmas before she died."

"She can hear you," I assured her.

Olivia began speaking. I relayed the message to Kelli. "She says you made her a picture frame with shells glued on from your trip to Florida a few summers ago. She said she loved it so much because she collected shells. She loved the pictures of you two from when she went on your family's vacation to California before that."

Kelli's jaw dropped in disbelief. "I don't know how you knew that."

"I told you. Olivia's here."

"Then ask her about our childhood," she insisted. "When we were in sixth grade, what did we promise we would grow up together and do?"

"She says you wanted to write poetry and publish song lyrics and that your pen names would be your childhood nicknames for each other, Kel-Kel and Livie."

She eyed me again like she still wasn't sure what to believe. "What did we do on her 13th birthday that we never told anyone about?"

"You went to the movies to celebrate, but when you got there, you realized you'd dropped your money somewhere along the way. You snuck into the movie without paying."

Kelli's lips curled up to hold back her tears, and her brows came together in sorrow. "Olivia?" She turned her head toward the ceiling and closed her eyes. "Livie, you're really here. God, I've missed you so much. I know you would have told me to stay away from Nate, to do something about it, and even though I had Justine by my side, I didn't have *you*. I needed you so badly." Her voice cracked. "There's so much I wanted to say over the past year. I wish you would have been here."

"She was," I said, translating. This only made Kelli cry harder.

"Tell her about the candle," Olivia said.

"What?" I replied, confused.

"Tell her I lit the candle to pray for her."

I nodded and took a deep breath in preparation to translate. "Kelli, Olivia wants you to know that the candle she lit, it was for you. She was praying for you."

With this, Kelli broke, sobbing uncontrollably and curling deeper into her ball.

I rubbed her arm for comfort again, continuing to relay Olivia's message. "And she says she hopes that you'll let your friends and family help you so that you can return to your old self. She doesn't want to see Nate hurt you anymore."

Kelli didn't speak for a few moments. Then she nodded slowly. "Okay. I promise. You've been my best friend forever, Olivia, but can you promise me that he won't hurt me anymore?"

"She says she'll be watching over you, like a guardian angel."

"Thank you," Kelli said. I wasn't sure if she was thanking me or Olivia.

I watched Olivia from behind Kelli. "Thank you so much for everything you've done, Crystal," Olivia said.

"I'm glad I could help," I replied out loud.

"Um, Crystal," Emma said. "I think we should go. I have a weird feeling."

"We will in a minute," I promised. *Put more faith in your friends. They might surprise you,* a thought surfaced in the back of my mind. *Is Emma being paranoid, or have her psychic exercises paid off?* I wondered.

Olivia jerked her head and looked at something behind her that even I couldn't see. "Emma's right. You have to leave," she told me. "Go. Go now. Tell Kelli I'll always be watching."

"I will," I promised as she faded. "She's gone."

"Gone?" Kelli asked softly.

"She said she'd always be watching, but we have to leave."

"Thank you," Kelli said one last time, her eyes sparkling. "What do we do now?"

"We keep you safe," Emma replied.

CHAPTER 27

When we exited the Owen's house, "safe" was not the first word that came to mind. Completely and utterly vulnerable was more like it. I nearly tumbled over a tall figure as I left the house. I stumbled backward in surprise.

"You," the figure snarled accusingly.

"Nate," I spat back.

He caught a glimpse of Kelli trailing behind me, and then his eyes fixated on me again. "I thought it was you I saw following Kelli here." His voice was anything but friendly. "I told you this ain't none of your business. I waited, but when you never came back, I came to make sure you weren't filling my girl's head with crazy ideas."

"You—you followed me?" Kelli asked in disbelief.

"Of course I did. I didn't want to go to that stupid festival, but I had to keep tabs on my girl."

Kelli shied back.

Stand up to him, Kelli, I thought. *Olivia once gave me courage. Let her do the same for you.*

With that thought, my prayer was answered. Kelli's posture changed, her eyes brightened, and she took a step forward. Kelli spoke in a tone that didn't seem like her own. "Kelli is not your *girl* anymore. You don't get to push people around like you do and expect something in return. You're a meaningless piece of crap that doesn't deserve someone as amazing as Kelli."

Olivia? I thought.

Nate shrank back in surprise. He took a second to digest what she'd just said, and then he reached for her. "Come on. We're leaving."

Kelli pulled away. "I'm not going anywhere with you!" This time it sounded like she was speaking for herself.

"Come on." The anger in his voice rose. "You can't be serious."

There were so many emotions thick in the air.

Kelli took a stand. "Oh, I am. Olivia showed me just how much of a jerk you are. If it wasn't for you, she might still be alive!" Something in her tone told me this was the key to everything.

"Olivia?" he practically shouted in confusion.

With that, Olivia appeared again, only this time she seemed more solid, more real. When I heard a gasp from everyone around me, I knew I wasn't the only one who could see her.

"What the—?" Nate's eyes widened. He took a few steps back and tripped over his own feet. He lay on the ground in terror. "No. It can't be. You're... you're... What the *hell*?"

Olivia advanced. A swirling wind consumed her, and I swore her eyes glowed red. "Leave my friend alone," she warned.

Nate raised his hands to shield himself.

Olivia continued moving toward him. "If you so much as

touch her again, I will make your life a *living hell*. Every step you take. Every corner you turn. I will be there waiting."

Nate whimpered.

My mouth was open in awe. *You go girl!*

"You come near my friend again—any of my friends, and that includes Crystal—you will regret it. For. The. Rest. Of. Your. Life."

Olivia's apparition charged at him again. He didn't waste another second. Nate scampered to his feet and ran off toward the street.

"Okay, okay," I heard him yelling back. "I swear it. I'll leave her alone."

Olivia turned to us and laughed. "That was fun."

Kelli's eyes fixated on Olivia. "Is that really you?" she asked slowly.

Olivia nodded.

"But... how?" Kelli asked.

"I don't know, to be honest. I've always been watching you, Kelli. I've always been here trying to help, but I think Crystal's the one to thank. I wouldn't be here like this without her here." Her gaze turned to me. "You have a really unusual gift, Crystal."

Tears sprung to Kelli's eyes. "Thank you. Thank you both for everything."

"My pleasure," Olivia responded. Then she turned as if she saw something the rest of us couldn't. "I think this is it for real this time."

"You have to go?" Kelli asked sadly.

Olivia nodded. "I can finally see the light. I don't think Nate is going to hurt you again. I think in all honesty he pissed his pants."

We all gave a chuckle.

"Will I see you again?" Kelli asked.

"I'll be here like always," Olivia promised.

Kelli didn't want to wait to go to the police station. She said she needed to talk about it while she still had the courage. I suggested that she bring someone with her, and because of how much I knew Justine cared, I convinced her to talk to Justine. She asked us to come along for the extra support, too.

I held onto the memory card on the way back to the park. There, we all went searched for Justine together.

I texted Derek.

We're done. You're off duty. We'll explain what happened later.

When we got to the kissing booth, though, Justine wasn't there. We walked up and down the rows of tents and booths looking for her.

"I'd text her," Kelli said, "but I know her phone doesn't fit in her costume."

We continued searching. As I was looking around, I spotted my mom.

"Hey," she waved. "I haven't seen you girls all night. Where are your wigs?"

"Um, they got itchy," Emma lied.

"Aren't you supposed to be fortune telling?" I asked.

"I took a 15 minute break. Why don't you come in, and I'll tell your fortune?"

"That's okay, Mom. Maybe another time."

"I'd like my fortune read," Kelli interjected, pushing her way past me toward my mom.

"Okay," my mom said. "You can go wait by my booth, and I'll be back in a few minutes."

"Sounds good." A small smile twitched at the edge of Kelli's lips.

Emma and I followed Kelli to the booth just to make sure we didn't lose each other in the throng of people. There was a "Back in 15 minutes" sign on the tent flap, so no one was waiting in line. My mom was back in a matter of minutes welcoming Kelli into the tent in a fake mystical voice.

In the bit of privacy we had, Emma's excitement finally burst. "I saw a ghost. A real ghost! I know it wasn't under the best of conditions, but it still happened." She beamed as if it was the coolest thing in the world.

I was about to tell her to calm down when I heard a familiar voice calling out to us. I turned to see a Cat in the Hat hat bouncing above the crowd. "How'd it go?" Derek asked once he reached us.

"Not as expected," I admitted.

"But pretty well," Emma finished. "Justine told Kelli about the video, and she showed up before us. I think we've convinced her to move on, and we're going to help her. Kelli's getting a reading right now, though." She gestured toward the tent.

"You know," Derek lowered his voice. "I've been wondering. Is your mom's fortune-telling booth, you know, real?"

Emma and I exchanged a glance. We giggled and nodded.

Derek raised his eyes. "Then I have some pretty good prospects for my future."

"You got your fortune read?" I asked.

"Yep."

"What'd she tell you?" I prodded curiously.

"You're the psychic. Figure it out."

I rolled my eyes at him. "It doesn't—"

"Work that way," he finished. "I know. I was just teasing." He nudged me. I was happy to have my problems solved and be back with my best friends, although we still had to find Justine and make it to the police station.

"So what'd you find out?" Emma asked Derek again, curious about his fortune.

Derek shrugged. "Just some good things about my romantic future."

Emma and I giggled together. "Your romantic future?" I asked. "You've never been romantic with anyone."

"Maybe I've just been waiting around for the right girl," he said, but he wouldn't meet either of our eyes.

Emma started to say something, but before she could, Kelli emerged from the tent with a smile. "Your mom says everything is going to be okay. Thank you."

To my surprise, Kelli pulled me into an embrace.

"No problem," I said. "Now let's go find Justine."

"I just saw her over by the apple bobbing booth," Derek announced, so we all took off together to look for her. Luckily, she'd stayed put since Derek last saw her. We waved her over from the end of the line.

She noticed Kelli first. "Kelli, are you okay?"

"Yeah, I'm..." She paused in search of the right word. "Fine. We found it, and they helped me." She pushed a strand of hair behind her ear nervously. "I'd like your support when I go to turn him in. You know, if you're not super mad at me for pushing you away."

Justine hugged Kelli. "That's great. I don't want to wait another minute. I'm so glad you've come to your senses."

We all piled into my mom's car again. With the memory card still securely hidden in my hand, Emma drove us to the police station.

"Thank you all so much for supporting me," Kelli said in the car. "I'm still scared to death, but after what you guys did and what your mom said, I think everything will be okay. I haven't felt this confident in a long time."

I felt prideful of her transformation, knowing full well that it was my translation of Olivia's words that had changed Kelli's mind.

We walked into the police station, and people were staring at us, probably perplexed by our costumes.

"Can I help you?" an officer who was walking through the main hall asked.

"We're just looking for Teddy," I said. "He's my mom's boyfr—I mean, fiancé."

"Oh, right," the guy said, pointing his finger at me in recognition. "You're the girl who started his nick name around here. Teddy Bear. Classic! He's at his desk." The officer turned and continued on his way.

When we reached Teddy's desk, he looked up from his paperwork, and his eyes filled with shock. "Crystal. Are you all okay?" His eyes shifted between each of us, searching for something that would indicate why we were here.

I set the small memory card down on his desk. I didn't know if he could actually use the video in a case since we obtained it illegally, but I wasn't sure that was the point of it anymore. Justine believed it was evidence, but Olivia wanted us to get the video to convince Kelli to get out of her relationship with Nate. I handed the card over anyway. "Um... this is evidence, and my friend Kelli would really like to talk to you about something. I need you to promise to keep her safe."

"I can do that," he promised. "What exactly is this about?"

"My boyfriend, sir," Kelli said.

Teddy nodded in understanding. "Kelli, do you mind having a seat over there?" Teddy pointed her toward some nearby chairs.

"I'd like Justine to stay with me," Kelli told him.

"Okay," he agreed kindly. "And you two," he pointed toward Emma and Derek, "do you mind if I have a word with my future step-daughter?"

Everyone left, leaving me to wonder what Teddy was planning to ask me. Was I in trouble? I took a seat across from him. He crossed his hands.

"Crystal, how did you get involved in this? You aren't friends with those girls, are you?"

I was momentarily stung by the accusation, as if I wasn't cool enough to hang out with popular girls, but I reminded myself how well he knew me and my friends.

I hung my head guiltily. "Justine asked me to help because she found out I was... you know." I lowered my voice even though everyone within ear shot already knew my secret. "Psychic."

"And did you use those abilities to help Kelli?"

I nodded. "I found the memory card."

He didn't ask where I'd found it like I'd expected but instead shifted through the folders piled on his desk.

I glanced back toward my best friends, who were waiting for me by the door.

Teddy opened one of the folders and pulled a photo from it, looking at it as he spoke.

"This girl went missing from her home recently. Her name is Hope Ross. Of course, we're working with some larger departments on the case, but no one has made much leeway. The first 48 hours are crucial in an investigation like this, and we've already hit that time limit, but we still don't know much. We don't even know if she's still alive, but we're hopeful. I was wondering if maybe you could help us crack the case."

He handed me the photo. When I took it, my heart fell to

the floor because I recognized the girl. It was a school photo, probably taken at the beginning of the school year, of a young girl around six years old with brown hair, freckles across her nose, and big chocolate eyes.

An image of her face as it was at that very moment flashed through my head. Her cheeks were full of color, but her eyes drooped in sadness. It was just a flash of her face telling me she was alive, and then it was gone. Unfortunately, it wasn't enough to give me any clue as to where she was.

My hands trembled as I set the photo back on the desk. My heart threatened to beat out of my chest.

"What?" Teddy asked. "What is it?"

I couldn't answer him at first. "You mean, you believe me?" I asked, my voice wavering. I knew he had accepted the idea, but I didn't think he actually *believed* it.

He paused for a moment as if pondering what to say. "Do you know why I'm a police officer, Crystal?"

I shook my head. He'd never told me why he entered the police force.

"I seem to have this strong sense of..." He paused in search of the right word. "Intuition. I'm good at solving cases. When I met your mother, I always suspected she had that same sense of intuition. It's what drew me to her. That, among other things."

I took in a sharp breath. Could Teddy have psychic abilities, too? My mom had said that the area had a rich history of psychics. I could hardly believe it, but that explained why he'd taken it so well.

"Unfortunately," he said, "my intuition is failing me on Hope's case. Do you think you can help?"

I paused for a moment, unsure. Then I nodded slowly. "I hope so. You'll have to give me some time, but I can tell you that I know she's still alive."

CHAPTER 28

*T*eddy thanked me, told me to enjoy the remaining few hours of the Halloween festival while he talked with Kelli, and sent me back to my friends. I asked Kelli if she wanted us to stay, but she told us we'd helped enough and that we should go enjoy ourselves.

Now that I had the issue of saving Kelli and Olivia off my chest, I felt like I deserved a good night out with my friends. I glanced back at Justine and Kelli as I exited the building, and I knew Kelli was going to be okay.

Emma drove us back to the park, and I worried about Hope the whole way. Emma noticed my nerves and encouraged me to just enjoy myself for one night. She was right. There wasn't anything I could do to help Hope right now anyway.

We walked up and down the aisles playing games and listening to the band play. We even took a walk down the haunted trail while Emma and I clung to Derek for protection, which honestly made me feel a bit safer even though the zombies were just volunteers in costume.

Sometime during the night, I cracked a real smile as I realized how much I'd accomplished in the last few hours. Kelli was okay and free from Nate, and Olivia had crossed over, which I hoped meant that her mom could move on, too.

I veered off from my best friends for a few minutes to visit my mom in her tent. She was standing outside waiting for her next victim.

"Maybe I could get a reading," I suggested.

"Or maybe I could get a reading from you," she joked, pulling back her tent flap and inviting me in. I walked into the small makeshift room, which was lit by electric candles since the coordinators agreed real candles could be potentially hazardous. There was a round table placed in the middle of the tent, one chair at the far end and one chair close to me. The table was covered with an appropriate table cloth, and her tarot cards and a crystal ball were sitting on top of it.

"Are you going to tell me where you really were all night?" she asked.

Of course, I thought. *She knows me far too well.*

"Just, um, some detective work," I managed to answer. It wasn't a lie, at least.

My mother looked at me like she didn't believe me.

I caved. "Okay, we didn't actually end up with the video last night. We went and got it today."

"You broke into Tammy's house to steal it?" She was disappointed.

A wave of guilt fell over me.

"Well, Derek says that since the door was unlocked, we didn't break in, and Emma says that since Olivia wanted us to have it, it wasn't stealing," I rationalized.

The look of disappointment was still painted on my

mother's face. "Crystal, you may have fantastic abilities, but you have to learn how to use them responsibly. Being psychic doesn't mean you're entitled to things other people aren't."

She was right.

"Okay," I agreed. "I understand, but I can't say I'm sorry. I may have saved Kelli's life."

My mother sighed. I wasn't sure if it was a sigh of defeat or because she couldn't accept my excuse.

I dropped my head in guilt, and my eyes fixated on the crystal ball as it called out to me.

"Mom!" I scolded. "Is that my crystal ball?"

"Yeah," she admitted as she took a seat across from me.

"But, why?" My face fell, hurt that she'd taken it from my room without asking.

She shrugged like it was no big deal. "I'm sorry. I figured that we owned one now, so I didn't have to borrow one from the shop."

"But it's mine," I said possessively, picking it up from its stand and pulling it close to me. It began glowing in my hands. I didn't look up to see if my mother noticed it, too; I was too consumed by the swirling colors pulling me in. I studied it intensely as its energy wrapped around me. I never knew what I saw in it, but after a moment, I quickly returned it to its stand.

"What?" my mom asked. "What did you see?"

"I—I don't know."

I didn't. All I knew was that it was about the little girl, the one with big chocolate eyes. I knew she needed help, and I knew she would be the focus of my next psychic adventure.

"Crystal, with everything I've seen you do, you have amazing abilities, which is surprising since just a few weeks ago I didn't think you had *any*. You're going to be a really amazing psychic."

Yeah, I thought, but I knew that being psychic wasn't ever going to be easy. I knew that from this moment on, I would never stop using my abilities to help people.

ABOUT THE AUTHOR

Alicia Rades is a USA Today bestselling author of young adult and new adult paranormal fiction. When she's not dreaming up magical stories, she's either binge-watching Netflix, meditating, or spending time with her family. She has an unhealthy obsession with psychic characters and writes with a deck of tarot cards next to her computer.